Byron Mac Cutcheon

Fitz-John Porter

Byron Mac Cutcheon

Fitz-John Porter

ISBN/EAN: 9783337401740

Printed in Europe, USA, Canada, Australia, Japan

Cover: Foto ©Raphael Reischuk / pixelio.de

More available books at **www.hansebooks.com**

FITZ-JOHN PORTER.

SPEECH

OF

HON. BYRON M. CUTCHEON,

OF MICHIGAN,

IN THE

HOUSE OF REPRESENTATIVES,

TUESDAY, FEBRUARY 16, 1886.

No man's opinion is worth more than his reasons are worth.

WASHINGTON.
1886.

SPEECH

OF

HON. BYRON M. CUTCHEON.

The House being in Committee of the Whole, and having under consideration the bill (H. R. 67) for the relief of Fitz-John Porter—

Mr. CUTCHEON said:

Mr. CHAIRMAN: Before proceeding with my remarks, I desire to say that the material I have before me is much greater than I can compress into the time allowed me; and for that reason I shall ask the courtesy and indulgence of my colleagues on the committee and other members of the House to permit me to pursue my argument without interruption until I have finished it; then, if any time should remain to me, or if any gentleman will yield me further time, I will gladly answer such questions as may be put to me, to the best of my ability.

I will state, Mr. Chairman, that the honorable gentlemen from Wyoming [Mr. CAREY], my colleague on the committee, has yielded me the remainder of his time, thirty-five minutes, which I desire first to occupy. He is now out of his seat, though he was here a moment ago; but that is the arrangement; so that I desire to proceed without break at the end of his time.

The CHAIRMAN. The Chair so understands.

Mr. CUTCHEON. Mr. Chairman, or perhaps I should say "if the court please," the supreme court-martial of the United States is now in session. We are engaged in rewriting history. It may be said that history, if wrong, should be rewritten. Let it be granted. But it should be rewritten at a time, upon evidence, and under circumstances that will be likely to assure greater and not less correctness.

Almost a quarter of a century has elapsed since the facts in this case were judicially investigated. The dust of years has gathered in the chambers of memory; boys have become men, men of middle age have become old, and many of them have passed on since then to—

> The undiscover'd country, from whose bourn
> No traveler returns.

Most of the conspicuous figures of that period who were connected with the events which led to Fitz-John Porter's conviction and dismissal have passed away. Halleck, who convened the court; Hunter, who presided; Garfield, who gave to the evidence his clear, strong, logical mind, and Lincoln, who approved the finding and sentence of the court, have all gone over to the majority. McDowell and McClellan, Hooker and Heintzelman, Burnside and Birney, Kearny and Reno and Grover, and hundreds of others, are no longer here to correct errors of fact or false constructions of evidence. At this distance of time and in this absence of witnesses we ought to proceed with the greatest caution in reversing their work.

General Fitz-John Porter, a colonel in the regular Army and major-general of volunteers, was, during the months of November and December, 1862, and January, 1863, fully, fairly, and patiently tried by a general court-martial, and, after every possible opportunity for defense, was convicted of disobedience of three several important and explicit orders from his commanding general, also of three separate specifications of misbehavior in the presence of the enemy, and was sentenced to be dishonorably dismissed from the service and disqualified for holding any office of profit or trust under the United States. The sentence was approved and executed. The latter part of the sentence has been removed by the exercise of the pardoning power. This bill is a legislative declaration of innocence.

I have no personal feeling in this cause, and no political bias, except in so far as the great names of Stanton, Garfield, and Lincoln would make me cautious to cast no shadow upon their probity or their integrity. This is a bill to set aside the finding and sentence of the highest court-martial ever assembled in this country, regularly constituted, convened by competent authority, bound by the sanction of a solemn oath, hearing and seeing the living witnesses, and assisted by the ablest counsel for the accused. The proceedings were reviewed by the able Judge-Advocate-General, approved and confirmed by the President, and carried duly into execution. Such a sentence, so approved, so executed, is beyond appeal. It is *res adjudicata* for all time. The President can not revoke it; the Supreme Court can not set it aside. He must be legislated into a pardon by the law-making power.

The very statement of the proposition would seem to be sufficient to show its impropriety. Not only that, he is to be rewarded, to be put back at the head of the list of colonels with rank the same as if he had not been dismissed.

It is at least an open question whether this bill as it stands will not also give him pay from the day of his dismissal. The bill provides—

That said Fitz-John Porter shall receive no pay, compensation, or allowance whatsoever prior to his appointment under this act.

That is to say he shall not receive the compensation prior to his appointment, but it does not say that after his appointment he shall not receive full compensation covering the period prior to his appointment. If this proviso is intended in good faith to exclude compensation covering the time prior to his appointment it should say so in unambiguous language.

Mr. Chairman, I am opposed to this bill—

First. Because I do not believe that Congress has constitutional power to reverse the finding of a general court-martial when it has been confirmed by the President of the United States and carried into execution by his order. The reasons for deciding that neither the President nor Congress can annul or set aside the final judicial judgment of a court-martial are given by Attorney-General Brewster in opinions of March 15, 1882, and June 23, 1884, from which last opinion are quoted extracts as follows:

A court-martial is to be respected in its judgments the same as any other court. Its findings, when rendered and approved according to the due forms of that law which creates it, are to be treated as would be the final judgments of a court of final jurisdiction in the law. * * * Such a judgment the President has no power to review and annul or set aside.

[See cited in the opinion of March 15, 1882, President Hayes's message of June 5, 1879; Dynes *vs.* Hooper, 20 Howard, 65; *Ex parte* Reed, 100 U. S. Rep., 13; Attorney-General's Opinions, volume 6, pages 370 and 507 (Cushing), volume 6, pages 170 and 274 (Legare and Nelson, volume 10, page 64, and volume 11, page 19 (Bates).]

Second. I do not believe that this House is qualified or fitted to review the finding of a judicial tribunal. It has none of the attributes of a court. It has none of the temper of a court. It has none of the sanctions of a court. It has none of the instrumentalities of a court. If courts-martial are a part of the judicial system, then this proposed action is usurpation of judicial powers. If they belong to the executive department as appurtenant to the Government and discipline of the Army, then it is usurpation of executive powers. In either case it is usurpation.

It is suggested that the United States, represented in Congress, has full power to remit a judgment in its favor. If it were a matter of civil damage, that perhaps would be true. But this is something more. It involves the reversal of a final verdict, involving only a question of guilt or innocence, and upon that I submit that none but a tribunal equipped to investigate that question can pass. It is not within the scope of legislative action.

Third. I am opposed to this bill because it is an invasion of the appointing power vested by the Constitution solely in the President.

If the President would be under obligation to regard the provisions of this bill, should it become law, then it would be tantamount to a legislative appointment—a violation of both the letter and spirit of the Constitution.

If he would not be bound to regard it as law, then it would be advice only—both an impertinence and a nullity.

If this can be done in one instance it can be done in all; and all the Legislature has to do is by act of Congress to abolish all offices, and then by another act create them, directing how they shall be filled, leaving to the Executive only the choice whether they shall remain vacant or be filled as dictated. We are therefore reduced to this dilemma: The bill in question is either advice or law. If it is advice, it is useless and without force; if it is law, it is usurpation of the executive prerogative. In either case it is inadvisable.

It is of no consequence that the present incumbent is willing to waive his prerogative, and to accept Congressional advice. The office is greater than the officer, and we have no right to degrade the former because the latter does not insist upon his rights.

Let us suppose for a moment that this House were in political accord with the Senate, and the Senate should to-morrow pass a bill increasing the number of Supreme Court judges to thirteen, and should designate four well-known Republican jurists to fill the four additional seats, so as to secure the political balance of that court for a long term of years, will it be contended that such an act would not be a trespass upon the prerogative of the Executive? But it would be no more so in principle than is this bill.

Fourth. I am opposed to the passage of this bill because I am profoundly convinced that the court-martial arrived at a just conclusion, under circumstances when both sides of the case were fully represented, at the only time when they were so represented; that their verdict was righteous and their sentence merciful.

It must be remembered that Fitz-John Porter does not stand before us with the presumption of innocence in his favor, as would be the case of a person standing before a jury at nisi prius. It is *res adjudicata.* He comes with the verdict of a competent court against him, and the presumption is in favor of the rightfulness of the decision of the court, and not in favor of the innocence of the accused. This is a point that seems to have been steadily overlooked in the argument on this question.

Before proceeding further with this branch of the subject I will give a hurried history of the military situation at that time. After the seven days' fighting around Richmond, General McClellan had changed the base of his operations from the Chickahominy to the James River, resting his right at Harrison's Landing on the river. General Pope had just been summoned from the West, where he had signalized his skill with marked success as a military man and soldier on several important occasions, and was intrusted with the command of an army then being formed from the corps of Generals Fremont, Banks, and McDowell, to be known as "the Army of Virginia" and consist of some thirty-odd thousand men. The purpose of this organization was, in the first place, to cover the approaches to Washington, and, secondly, to demonstrate in favor of McClellan in the direction of Richmond. General Pope assumed command of this consolidated force in the latter days of June, 1862, and his first step was to unite the force under him and move forward, with his right at Sperryville, while McDowell's corps was moved forward to Waterloo Bridge, the whole force being along the line and in front of the Rappahannock.

Now from this time on, the whole purpose of the Government at Washington was to consolidate the Army of the Potomac with the Army of Virginia. How should it be done? To withdraw Pope from his position on the Rappahannock in order to form a junction with the army operating on the James River was impossible, because it would have left the national capital uncovered. McClellan was then calling for re-enforcements, his first call being for one hundred thousand men, which was subsequently modified by a call for fifty thousand; but as his ultimatum, he said, he could not advance on Richmond with less than thirty-five thousand men. The Secretary of War looked over the entire field endeavoring to find from what point he could gather these re-enforcements to send McClellan, and finally it was determined that there was no other resource than to unite the two armies, that of the Potomac and of the Army of Virginia, in front of Washington and upon the line of the Rappahannock.

Upon the 3d of August, 1862, McClellan was directed to withdraw immediately the Army of the Potomac from its position on the James and interpose it between Washington and Richmond. This movement began on the 18th of August. Porter's corps, or one of his divisions, I believe, was the first to embark, and Heintzelman's, Reno's, and one or two other divisions were transferred from the James to the Army of Virginia prior to the operations about to be referred to.

Halleck, who was then the General-in-Chief of all the armies, directed General Pope to cling to the line of the Rappahannock. He telegraphed him again and again, "If you can but hold on until the 25th we shall re-enforce you all you need." Again he telegraphed on the 26th to Pope ordering him "to hold every inch of ground and fight like the devil." And, Mr. Chairman, Pope did fight like the devil, for he was always ready for a fight. So Pope with his army held his position on the line of the Rappahannock, with his left at the fords above Fredericksburg, where he was joined by Porter's divisions. This was the situation on the night of the 26th, when Pope ordered Porter's command to join him the next day.

Up to this time he had been under the direct command of the General-in-Chief. On the morning of the 27th General Porter with his command arrived at Warrenton Junction and reported to Pope; but meanwhile, on the 13th of August, General Lee cut himself loose from Richmond, leaving it with only one army corps, or rather one division, that of D. H. Hill, and leaving it for McClellan to work his will with as he would, or dared, swung out into Virginia, concentrating his force at Gordonsville, with Jackson in advance and Longstreet following Jackson, and by the 18th of August the whole confederate army was reunited opposite the Federal army on the Rappahanock with the design of crushing the small army opposed to him before a junction of the Union armies could be effected, and then pushing on to Washington.

A fortunate rise in the river prevented him from making his contemplated movement upon Pope to crush him before the troops from the Army of the Potomac could reach him. But the rise in the river which saved Pope, temporarily separated one division of Lee's army from his command. At the suggestion of Jackson upon the 25th, Jackson was to make his contemplated move around the right of the Federal Army by way of Jefferson to Salem and Rectortown to Gainesville, plunge down through the gap on Pope's right and rear, cut his line of communications, capture his supplies, and get between him and the national capital.

With some reluctance, as I understand, General Lee assented to this arrangement. On the 25th Jackson marched from Jefferson to Salem. On the next day, the 26th, he struck out from Salem by way of White Plains and by Thoroughfare Gap to Gainesville, through Gainesville to Catlett's and Bristoe. A little after dark, having marched 30 miles without rest, he struck Pope's communications in rear and captured two trains of cars. And before midnight Stuart and Trimble were at Manassas Junction, 36 miles and more from where they had started in the morning. That shows what generals can do when they are in earnest. That was what the men we regarded as on the wrong side and supporting a bad cause could accomplish when they were commanded by a general who was determined to accomplish the purpose he had in view.

Jackson struck the railroad on the night of the 26th in the neighborhood of Kettle Run, a little tributary of Broad Run, which comes down between Bristoe and Catlett's Station. Pope found his telegraph communications cut and thought it was Jeb Stuart raiding in his rear. He put some regiments on flat cars and ran them down there, to find General Ewell with an entire division. Immediately old fighting Joe Hooker with his division was sent down; and on the afternoon of the 27th the battle raged, until three hundred of Hooker's men lay dead or wounded on the field.

Where at this time was Porter? He had just reported to General Pope that forenoon at Warrenton Junction. The first order that cuts any figure in this case is the order of the evening of the 27th, 6.30 p. m. It has been claimed that this order was an entirely unimportant, immaterial order. Now, let us see as to that. As the gentleman from Alabama [Mr. WHEELER] has very properly said, orders are always given with a purpose.

General Pope and his subordinate officers met that evening and talked over the situation, and orders for the operations of next morning were issued. What was the situation? Jackson was upon the railroad between Bristoe and Manassas and at Manassas; McDowell and Reno and Sigel were west of Gainesville, between Jackson and Thoroughfare Gap, the only road by which Longstreet could come to his succor. Porter was at Warrenton Junction, 9 miles from Hooker's battlefield. Hooker was at Bristoe late in the evening.

Now, what was the purpose of the orders for the next day? To concentrate Pope's army on the two sides of Jackson, one half on the north and west, the other on the south and west, and to pen Jackson between these two armies, McDowell, Reno, and Sigel coming from the direction of Gainesville, and Porter, Kearny, and Hooker coming from the west, with Banks in their rear. With this purpose Pope issued his orders. The first order to Fitz-John Porter is as follows:

HEADQUARTERS ARMY OF VIRGINIA,
Bristoe Station, August 27, 1862—6.30 p. m.

Maj. Gen. F. J. PORTER, *Warrenton Junction:*

GENERAL: The major-general commanding directs that you *start at 1 o'clock to-night and come forward with your whole corps, or such part of it as is with you, so as to be here by daylight to-morrow morning. Hooker has had a very severe action with the enemy, with a loss of about three hundred killed and wounded.* The enemy has been driven back, but is retiring along the railroad. *We must drive him from Manassas*, and clear the country between that place and Gainesville, where McDowell is. If Morell has not joined you, send him word to push forward immediately; also send word to Banks to hurry forward with all speed to take your place at Warrenton Junction. *It is necessary on all accounts that you should be here by daylight.* I send an officer with this dispatch who will conduct you to this place. Be sure to send word to Banks, who is on the road from Fayetteville, probably in the direction of Bealeton. Say to Banks, also, that he had best run back the railroad trains to this side of Cedar Run. If he is not with you, write him to that effect.

By command of General Pope:

GEORGE D. RUGGLES,
Colonel and Chief of Staff.

What was he wanted for? Stonewall Jackson, one of the most brilliant generals this century has produced since Napoleon, was in Pope's rear, and had been fighting Hooker's division, which that evening had lost three hundred men killed and wounded. The battle was to be renewed in the morning, and as Heintzelman swears, he had informed Pope before dark that Hooker's division was out of ammunition—that there were not more than five rounds to each man—there was an emergency. Stonewall Jackson was between the upper and nether millstones. He could not retreat westward, because McDowell, Reno, and Sigel were on that side; nor in the direction of Warrenton Junction, because Porter, Hooker, Kearny, and Banks were there. Which way was he to go? Pope figured out the situation, and thought the only way Jackson could escape was to turn his right and move to the south of the Orange and Alexandria Railroad. The object of Pope was to concentrate these three army corps upon him at daylight before he could get away. Here is the order to General Kearny, dated at 9 p. m.:

HEADQUARTERS, BRISTOE, *August* 27, 1862—9 p. m.

Major-General KEARNY:

At the earliest blush of dawn push forward with your command with all speed to this place. You can not be more than 3 or 4 miles distant. Jackson, A. P. Hill, and Ewell are in front of us. *Hooker has had a severe fight with them to-day. McDowell marches upon Manassas Junction from Gainesville to-morrow at daybreak; Reno upon the same place at the same hour. I want you here at day-dawn, if possible, and we shall bag the whole crowd.* Be prompt and expeditious, and never mind wagon trains or roads till this affair is over. Lieutenant Brooks will deliver you this communication. He has one for General Reno and one for General McDowell. Please have these dispatches sent forward instantly by a trusty staff officer, who will be sure to deliver them without fail, and make him bring back a receipt to you before daylight. Lieutenant Brooks will remain with you and bring you to this camp. Use the cavalry I send you to escort your staff officer to McDowell and Reno.

JNO. POPE,
Major-General, Commanding.

Not only that, but at 9 p. m., this to Major-General McDowell:

HEADQUARTERS ARMY OF VIRGINIA,
Bristoe Station, August 27, 1862—9 p. m.

Major-General McDOWELL:

At daylight to-morrow morning march rapidly on Manassas Junction with your whole force, resting your right on the Manassas Gap Railroad, throwing your left well to the east. Jackson, Ewell, and A. P. Hill are between Gainesville and Manassas Junction. We had a severe fight with them to-day, driving them back several miles along the railroad. If you will march promptly and rapidly at the earliest dawn of day upon Manassas Junction we shall bag the whole crowd. *I have directed Reno to march from Greenwich at the same hour upon Manassas Junction, and Kearny, who is in his rear, to march on Bristoe at daybreak. Be expeditious, and the day is our own.*

JNO. POPE,
Major-General, Commanding.

Here was a strategic combination, three army corps concentrating upon a single point, to surround Jackson at daylight before he could get away, and the whole key of the situation was in the hands of Fitz-John Porter at Warrenton Junction. Therefore General Pope gave him this order:

Major-General PORTER:

Start at 1 o'clock to-night, and come forward with your whole corps, or with so much as is with you, so as to be here at daylight to-morrow morning. It is of the last importance that you should be here at daylight.

That was the tenor of the dispatch. General Pope knew that everything depended upon absolute promptness. Warrenton Junction is 9 miles from Bristoe Station. The intervening space is a broad, open, pine plain—Manassas plain. I see gentlemen sitting around me who have marched over it again and again, and who know its character. It was an open pine plain, with no fences or obstructions of any kind, with the exception of one or two small streams; and roads everywhere. What did Porter do? He received this imperative order to start at 1 o'clock. General Sykes and General Morell, his division commanders, and General Butterfield, one of his brigade commanders, were in the tent with him. Holding the dispatch in his hand, he said, "Gentlemen, there is something for you to sleep on." They stepped out of the lighted tent into the starlight. The night appeared to be dark, and somebody said that it would not be possible to march at 1 o'clock. Then, after a little conversation, in which General Sykes swears positively the tenor of the order was never mentioned—nothing except that it was an order to march at 1 o'clock, nothing about the imperative terms of the order—Porter said, "Very well, we will march at 3 o'clock." Now the evidence is that they did not march at 3 o'clock. The reveille was sounded at 3 o'clock, but it was broad daylight, and the sun was up, before they were well upon the road. It was half past 10 before they reached Bristoe Station; it was half past 2 in the afternoon, as testified by one of the brigade commanders, before their rear reached Bistoe, and of course by that time Jackson was far away.

What are the excuses offered for Porter's disobedience of this order?

First, that the night was dark and that he could not march. Yet that very night, and at that very hour, Stonewall Jackson, having burned our supplies at Manassas, marched two of his divisions to Centreville and a third, Taliaferro's, marched by the Sudley road to the old Bull Run battle-ground, nearly 9 miles, and bivouacked next morning at Sudley Ford. In fact, the whole rebel army marched that night. The same night McDowell was on the march; part of Reno's division was on the march. I believe every division of the Union Army, except Porter's, was on the march during some part of that night. But Porter could not march! Worse than that, he never attempted to march. Why, if the night was dark so that his progress would be impeded, what ought he to have done? The point of the order given him by General Pope was that he should be at Bristoe Station at daylight. Therefore, if the night was dark, instead of starting later than the hour indicated in the order, he should have started earlier. He should have said, "Gentlemen, we are to be at Bristoe Station at daylight. I do not know what it means, but there must be some emergency, or the commanding general would not have given this order; so you had better get ready to start right away, because the night is dark, and if there should be wagons on the road it will take us longer than if the circumstances were favorable."

Mr. BROWN, of Pennsylvania. May I interrupt the gentleman a moment?

Mr. CUTCHEON. Certainly.

Mr. BROWN, of Pennsylvania. The gentleman forgets that a big thunder-shower was manufactured in this House two years ago as an additional excuse for Porter's failure to obey that order. [Laughter on the Republican side.]

Mr. CUTCHEON. We will let that thunder-shower pass over for the present. I will go on in spite of the rain.

Mr. HOPKINS. I would like to ask the gentleman from Michigan [Mr. CUTCHEON] whether that thunder-storm was ever heard of before it appeared in this House two years ago?

Mr. CUTCHEON. I believe not. I believe the gentleman from Pennsylvania [Mr. BROWN] is right about that; that was home-made thunder.

The next excuse is that Porter's troops were fatigued with their day's march. They were the freshest troops in the Army. Sykes's division had been in camp since the forenoon, and Morell's division had mostly arrived before sundown. But even if they had been tired, even tired troops must march in an emergency. The third excuse is that there were wagons on the road. The officer who brought the order swears that he passed the last wagon at Catlett's Station, and as the wagons were going in the same direction, he would not have encountered them before daylight. The excuse is a paltry one. It is one that no soldier who was in earnest ought to have made. If wagons were in the road he should have put them out of the road. Porter was found guilty of disobedience of the order to march at 1 o'clock.

EVENTS OF AUGUST 29.

On the morning of the 29th, at 3 a. m., General Pope sends this order:

HEADQUARTERS ARMY OF VIRGINIA,
Near Bull Run, August 29, 1862—3 a. m.

GENERAL: McDowell has intercepted the retreat of Jackson. Sigel is immediately on the right of McDowell. Kearny and Hooker march to attack the enemy's rear at early dawn. Major-General Pope *directs you to move upon Cen-*

treville at the first dawn of day with your whole command, leaving your trains to follow. It is very important that you should be here at a very early hour in the morning. A severe engagement is likely to take place, and your presence is necessary.

I am, general, very respectfully, your obedient servant,

GEORGE D. RUGGLES,
Colonel and Chief of Staff.

Major-General PORTER.

The purpose of the campaign of the 29th was to hem Jackson in between Gainesville and Centreville before Longstreet should arrive. Heintzelman and Reno ordered forward in pursuit; Reynolds and Sigel on the south to attack at dawn; Porter ordered to close the gap on the west.

"A severe engagement is likely to take place," General Pope says. Did Porter obey that order, as a good soldier should; and if not, why not? I will answer that question. By the testimony it appears that that order reached Porter between daylight and sunrise. It was daylight at 4 in the morning, and the sun rose at 5.26. That order reached Porter between daylight and sunrise, yet at 7 o'clock he was still in his quarters back in front of Bristoe Station. At 6 o'clock that morning he was writing a dispatch, which I will presently read.

I may as well here as anywhere allude to

PORTER'S ANIMUS TOWARD POPE.

When he was ordered to join Pope he telegraphed on August 26 to General Burnside, telling him of his movements, and added, "Inform McClellan, that I may know that I am doing right." He wanted to know whether he was doing right in obeying an order from his superior officer to report to his commanding general! He had been ordered to join General Pope, yet he wanted McClellan to tell him whether he was doing right or not!

Immediately after joining Pope at Warrenton Junction, on the 27th of August, Porter telegraphed to General Burnside as follows:

* * * Everything here is *at sixes and sevens*, and I find I am *to take care of myself in every respect.* Our line of communication *has taken care of itself in compliance with orders.* * * * No guard accompanying trains and small ones guard bridges.

Again, on the same afternoon, before receiving the order to march to Bristoe, he telegraphed to Burnside:

AUGUST 27, 1862—4 p. m.

GENERAL BURNSIDE: * * * "I hear that they [Pope's troops] are *much demoralized* and needed some good troops to give them heart, *and, I think, head.* We are *working now to get behind Bull Run*, and I presume will be there in a few days, *if strategy don't use us up. The strategy is magnificent*, and the *tactics in inverse ratio.*" * * * I do not doubt the enemy have a large amount of supplies *provided for them*, and I believe they have *a contempt for the Army of Virginia. I wish myself away from it, with all our old Army of the Potomac*, and so do our *companions.*"

The next morning after his leisurely arrival at Bristoe Station, he telegraphs:

All that talk about taking Jackson, &c., *was bosh.* * * * The story of McDowell having cut off Longstreet *was without foundation.* I expect the next thing will be a raid on our rear *by Longstreet, who was "cut off."*

On the morning of the 29th, at about 3 a. m., Porter was ordered to move on Centreville "at the first dawn of day." The sun rose that morning at 5.26. At 6 o'clock, as I have said, Porter was still in his quarters, engaged in writing the following loyal dispatch to General Burnside:

BRISTOE, 29—6 a. m.

To General BURNSIDE:

* * * * * * *

Heintzelman and Reno are at Centreville, where they marched yesterday, and Pope went to Centreville *with the last two as a body-guard*, at the time *not knowing where was the enemy*, and when Sigel was fighting within 8 miles of him and within sight. *Comment is unnecessary.* * * * *I hope Mac. is working and will soon get us out of this.* (Volume 1, page 377.)

I have been assured by a gentleman, a resident of this city, then commanding a regiment of Kearny's division, that General Birney, then commanding a brigade of Kearny's division, heard Porter say on the morning of the 28th that "he would not put his corps into battle to be slaughtered for such d—d fool as John Pope."

Again, on August 29, Porter, in reply to an inquiry from Col. T. C. H. Smith, ordnance officer, whether he had received his ammunition, said that it was "going where it belonged;" that it was "on the road to Alexandria, where we are all going." That meant: "We are not going to use any ammunition here; we are not going to have any fighting. It is all going where it belongs—where McClellan is."

(See also testimony of Surgeon William L. Faxon, Thirty-second Massachusetts, proceedings of board, page 844.) He says:

As I crossed the run [at Bristoe] I heard General Porter make this remark: "Go tell Morell to halt his division. I don't care a damn if I don't get there."

Mr. BRAGG. Will the gentleman permit me to ask him a question? Did not this same Surgeon Faxon, who heard that wonderful remark, describe the man who made it as wearing a major-general's uniform; and was it not proven that General Porter, at that time, never had worn a major-general's uniform, and had not one with him at all? That all appears in the evidence.

Mr. CUTCHEON. It may be so. I will allow the gentleman to answer that question in his own time.

This fairly exhibits the spirit of dislike, distrust, contempt, and insubordination which Porter indulged toward Pope. Nor was he alone in it. McClellan appears to have been in sympathy with Porter. At 3.30 p. m., August 29, he telegraphed Halleck:

I am clear that one of two courses must be adopted. First, to concentrate all our available forces and *open communication* with Pope, and *second, to leave Pope to get out of his scrape, &c., at once* using all our means to make the capital safe.

And again, to Halleck:

I have no confidence in the dispositions made as I gather them. To speak frankly, and the occasion requires it, there appears to be a *total absence of brains.*

It is in the light of this spirit of insubordination that we must interpret Porter's conduct on the 28th and 29th of August, 1862.

The second order on the 29th to Porter was brought by General Gibbon in person, and delivered at the Weir house.

It was as follows:

HEADQUARTERS ARMY OF VIRGINIA,
Centreville, August 29, 1862.

Push forward with your corps and King's division, which you will take with you, *upon Gainesville.* I am following the enemy down the Warrenton turnpike. Be expeditious or we will lose much.

JOHN POPE,
Major-General, Commanding.

How came Gibbon to bring this order? There are gentlemen here who were with Gibbon the night before at Groveton. Coming down the Warrenton pike from the west a little before dusk, leading McDowell's corps, being ordered to move on Centreville, Gibbon ran into the right of Stonewall Jackson's command. . A fierce action ensued, in which Gibbon lost several hundred men.

Mr. BRAGG. Seven hundred and seventy out of his four regiments.

Mr. CUTCHEON. I think the gentleman is correct. He was there, and knows. After the fight was over, General King, at 1 o'clock that night, withdrew the corps from the Warrenton pike, near Groveton, and came down to Manassas Junction. Gibbon, who had made the fight, knew that this had opened the door for Longstreet to join Jackson, the very thing he knew General Pope did not wish to happen. General Gibbon mounted his horse and rode with all speed by way of Manassas Junction to Centreville—with such speed that he broke down his horse and had to have a relay with which to return. He there had a conference with Pope; explained the situation; explained King's withdrawal from the Warrenton pike, and how the door had been opened for Longstreet. General Pope then gave him the order to Porter which I have just read:

Push forward with your corps and King's division, which you will take with you, upon Gainesville. I am following the enemy down the Warrenton pike. Be expeditious, or we will lose much.

Gibbon with that order galloped at full speed, met Porter about 8 o'clock a. m. at the Weir house, near Manassas Junction, and delivered the order to Porter. At that time Porter had left his bivouac near Bristoe. The head of Sykes's division was at the station, right where the cars were burned, as witnesses have testified. The head of Morell's division had just got up to the turning point where the Gainesville road turns from the Bristoe Station road, about a mile west from Manassas. Immediately orders were sent back to halt the column. Sykes was already halted. Morell, I think, was halted also. To save the time of countermarching Sykes's division, Morell was ordered to proceed at once on the Gainesville road and Sykes to follow. The march proceeds for about 4 miles, when they arrive at a small stream, or rather the bed of a stream, known as Dawkin's Branch. It was now about 11 o'clock in the morning. Porter's corps consisted of Morell's division, Sykes's division of regulars, Piatt's brigade, and thirty-six pieces of artillery. Arriving at Dawkin's Branch, the column halted. Right there they met a horseman, who had just come from Gainesville over the road, and reported the road clear, but the enemy's skirmishers at Gainesville. A conference took place. Some skirmishers were sent forward across the branch. A few scattering shots were fired from along the woods, perhaps a thousand yards in advance of Porter's head of column. Warren closed up his brigade *en masse* on the left of the road.

Mr. BROWN, of Pennsylvania. Will the gentleman explain what is the distance from Gainesville to Dawkin's Branch?

Mr. CUTCHEON. About 5 miles. Morell deployed Griffin's brigade to the right of the road. Warren, as I have said, was massed on the left. Two companies were deployed at the front as skirmishers. Porter and Morell had been there about half an hour deliberating what further they would do when General McDowell came to the front of the column bearing an order he had just received from General Pope—

which order, by the way, Porter had already received. That order was as follows, known as the joint order:

[General Orders, No. 5.]

HEADQUARTERS ARMY OF VIRGINIA,
Centreville, August 29, 1862.

Generals McDOWELL and PORTER:

You will please move forward *with your joint commands toward Gainesville. I sent General Porter written orders to that effect an hour and a half ago.* Heintzelman, Sigel, and Reno are moving on the Warrenton turnpike, and must be not far from Gainesville. I desire that *as soon as communication is established between this force and your own the whole command shall halt.* It may be necessary to fall back behind Bull Run, at Centreville, to-night. I presume it will be so on account of our supplies. I have sent no orders of any description to Ricketts, and none to interfere in any way with the movements of McDowell's troops, except what I sent by his aid-de-camp last night, which were to hold his position on the Warrenton pike until the troops from here should fall upon the enemy's flank and rear. I do not even know Ricketts's position, as I have not been able to find out where General McDowell was until a late hour this morning. General McDowell will take immediate steps to communicate with General Ricketts, and instruct him to rejoin the other divisions of his corps as soon as practicable. If any considerable advantages are to be gained by departing from this order it will not be strictly carried out. One thing must be had in view, that the troops must occupy a position from which they can reach Bull Run to-night or by morning. The indications are that the whole force of the enemy is moving in this direction at a pace that will bring them here by to-morrow night or next day. My own headquarters will be for the present with Heintzelman's corps or at this place.

JOHN POPE,
Major-General, Commanding.

The disobedience of this order was the second specification of the first charge.

Now, right here is about the only time I wish to refer at all to this map. Here [illustrating] is Warrentown pike, extending in a southwesterly direction from Centreville to Gainesville. Here is the Alexandria and Orange Railroad; this is the Manassas Gap Railroad, extending northwesterly from Manassas to Gainesville. They form a junction here at Gainesville, at an acute angle. Here were Heintzelman and Reno, moving upon the Warrenton pike from Centreville westward. Here was Fitz-John Porter, half way between Manassas and Gainesville, facing northwesterly. Jackson's line extended in a southwesterly direction from Sudley Ford to the turnpike west of Groveton. Here were the Union forces fronting them. Here were Reno, Hooker, and Sigel on the Union right, and Reynolds on the extreme left, at the Lewis house. Here was Morell, at Dawkin's Branch. Here was Sykes, stretched along the road back to Bethlehem church. Here was McDowell, extending along the road back toward Manassas; and Ricketts was off here extending back toward Bristoe. That was the situation at 11 o'clock. Now, what was the object of General Pope? It was to have General Porter advance upon this Gainesville road until his right had reached out and grasped hands with Reynolds, who was here between the Lewis house and Groveton [illustrating]. Now, what was in front of him? So far as he knew, nothing in the world but skirmishers. General Warren, a good friend of Porter's, testified as follows, on page 83 of volume 2 of the proceedings of the Schofield board:

Q. So far as you know was there an enemy in that position at that time?

A. We could see as far as the woods allowed us. We could see them along the edges of the woods. There was no knowing whether they were in force or not. We should have had to make a demonstration to find out what it was. I know very often we did not see the enemy's line of battle when it was very heavy.

* * * * * * *

Q. You did not know what force of the enemy was in your front?

A. No; I did not know how great they were. I knew there was a force.
Q. You saw enough there to make you cautious in your movements?
A. Yes. In making a military maneuver no man is justified in going upon the uncertainties of the occasion. If he does not know what force is in his front he should make an effort to develop it.

That is what I say; that is what it seems to me every soldier ought to say—if you do not know what force is in your front you ought to make a movement to develop the enemy's force and find out.

But I must press on, as I see my time is short.

Porter had been advised by the 3 a. m. order that a battle was expected; that Hooker and Kearny were to attack; that Sigel was on their left to extend the line. He knew the purpose of his march on Gainesville was to unite his right with Reynolds's left—that his order was to advance until communication was established. He was to fight if need be. This communication was not established. No *bona fide* attempt was made to establish it.

After the brief interview (not exceeding fifteen minutes) between Porter and McDowell, in which McDowell said, "Put your troops in here, and I will take mine and go to the right," Porter, instead of remaining at the front at Dawkin's Branch, left the head of his column, went 2⅜ miles to the rear, lay down in the shade by Bethlehem church, and remained there until dark. He never visited the head of his column again that day until it was dark. I defy refutation of this statement.

I say, then, that this absolute absence of vigor, this complete lack of attempt to carry out his order, his retirement from the head of his column to Bethlehem church, where he could neither see nor hear nor know what was going on, his inaction while the sounds of battle were constantly throbbing in his ears, can only be explained upon the hypothesis of a want of good faith, a purpose "to let Pope get out of his scrape" as best he could. Thus far, from the moment he joined Pope, he had not promptly and in a soldierly manner obeyed one solitary order that he had received from his commander.

He had acted upon the order to march to Bristoe in his own time and in his own manner. When he received the order to march on Centreville "at the first dawn of day" to take part in a battle, he was an hour after sunrise still in his tent writing captious dispatches and wishing that "Mac will soon get us out of this."

When, at 9 a. m., he is ordered to fill his cartridge-boxes he says, indifferently, to Colonel Smith, that the ammunition "was where it belonged;" it "was on its way to Alexandria, where we are all going." At Dawkin's Branch he said, "we can't go in there anywhere without getting into a fight."

His whole demeanor manifested the most utter want of earnestness or desire for the success of the army. His whole correspondence with Burnside showed that he did not regard that as his army; that he wanted to be away from it; that he had a most hearty dislike for its commander; that he looked to "Mac" as his patron, monitor, and favorite. What attempt did he make to cross over to Sigel? If any gentleman can tell me of any I shall be glad. I am told that Griffin moved his brigade six hundred yards to the right. So he did. He deployed this brigade, a magnificent brigade, and moved to the right until the head of column reached some pine bushes, when somebody said, "You can not get through there," and immediately he halted his column, faced about, and went into the brush at Dawkin's Branch. That was the only attempt to connect with the right.

Porter's process of reasoning was a simple one. If Pope gains the prestige of a victory, then Pope will command the united armies. If Pope is beaten, then the army must fall back within the lines of Washington, Pope will be a failure, and "McClellan's star" will shine out once more.

His reasoning was not only simple, it was sound, as the sequel too surely proved.

He was found guilty of disobedience to the "joint order;" but thus far he could make a show of excuse for his disobedience: he was out of the presence of his commander; the discretion allowed to a corps commander; obstacles in the way of a strict obedience, and other excuses. But

THE 4.30 ORDER

changed all this. It was given on the very field of battle. It was given by his immediate commander under circumstances when the subordinate had but one duty, and that was to obey at once, fully, and with all his energy.

That order was as follows:

HEADQUARTERS IN THE FIELD,
August 29—4.30 p. m.

Major-General PORTER:

Your line of march brings you in on the enemy's right flank. *I desire you to push forward into action at once* on the enemy's flank, and, if possible, on his rear, keeping your right in communication with General Reynolds. The enemy is massed in the woods in front of us, but can be shelled out *as soon as you engage their flank.* Keep heavy reserves and *use your batteries, keeping well closed to your right all the time.* In case you are obliged to fall back, do so to your right and rear, so as to keep you in close communication with the right wing.

JOHN POPE,
Major-General, Commanding.

All that afternoon the roar of battle was sounding in his ears, or at least it would have been had he not been 2½ miles from the head of his own column.

Here was an imperative order, an order to attack. It admitted of no misconstruction. There was no discretion. If a battle was raging, there was no recourse but to obey at once.

McDowell says, speaking of the time he was conferring with Porter, before 12 o'clock:

The sound of battle, which seemed to be at its height on our right toward Groveton. (G. C. M., 83 [85].)

* * * * * * *

Q. Was or not the battle raging at that time?

A. The battle *was raging on our right.* That is, if you regard that road from Bethlehem church to Gainesville to be substantially northwest, the *battle was raging* to the right and east of that line. (G. C. M. [86] 85.)

If no battle was raging, it was equally imperative.

A new excuse must be found. It was found.

The excuse was that the order was received too late for execution. Now, Mr. Chairman, how much of my time remains?

The CHAIRMAN. The gentleman has forty-five minutes of his time remaining.

Mr. CUTCHEON. I find I must hurry on.

The order was dispatched from Stone house at 4.30. It was borne by Capt. Douglas Pope, a staff officer. The distance to Bethlehem church was just 5 miles. He swears he believes he delivered it by 5 o'clock. (G. C. M., page 60.) The course of subsequent events shows that it must have been delivered as early as 5.30. Charles Duffer, or derly, says about 5.30, (G. C. M., page 201). Archelaus Dyer, First Ohio, puts it at 5.15. (Board proceedings, page 1097.)

Warren's dispatch, dated at 5.45 (Board proceeding, page 81), which says, "I met then an orderly from General Porter to General Morell, saying he must push on and press the enemy," shows that the order must have been received by 5.30.

There is no doubt whatever that the order General Warren speaks of, which had already reached him before 5.45, was the very order sent to Morell to make the attack in obedience to the 4.30 order. Warren says:

5.45 p. m. August 29, 1862, I received an order to go to the support of Morell. I faced about and did so.

The sun set that evening at 6.36 o'clock. When the order was received the sun was an hour high. This was 5.45. Already the order had reached Porter at Bethlehem church; already it had been carried 2 miles to the front, and had reached the front before sunset that night at 6.36, fully an hour before sunset.

Mr. BRAGG. Permit me to ask the gentleman a question.

Mr. CUTCHEON. Certainly.

Mr. BRAGG. Colonel Locke went forward with the order that he received—that 4.30 order.

Mr. CUTCHEON. I understand all about that.

Mr. BRAGG. That 4.30 order, as subsequent dispatches brought by General McDowell himself at West Point dated at 6.30 showed, that order had not been received by Porter at all.

Allow me to say the testimony shows that two witnesses stated subsequently they did not know anything about the time they delivered the order.

Mr. CUTCHEON. With all due respect to the gallant commander of the Iron Brigade, and we love him for the enemies he has made [laughter and applause], I want to say there were three orders to attack that went to Morell that afternoon. First, the written order of General Porter to push out two regiments supported by two others to attack the party with the section of artillery in front. That was late in the afternoon. What did General Porter then suppose was in his front? He says "the party with a section of artillery in front."

General Morell says nothing was ever done under that order. The next order was a verbal one carried by Colonel Locke to General Morell to make preparation for attack. That was followed up by a written order, carried by an orderly, to attack.

It was a written order. It was not a verbal order. He could not read a verbal order. It was the written order carried by an orderly when there was a full hour before sunset. [Applause on the Republican side.]

Mr. BRAGG. The gentleman should read the documents before him.

Mr. CUTCHEON. I have read three thousand pages of this evidence, and I think I know what I am talking about all the time. Morell was already deployed, or partly so. The skirmishers were already out and in contact with the enemy. Warren was massed on the left of the road behind the branch. The batteries, or some of them, were already in position to cover the advance. Wilcox, of Longstreet's corps, with his division, had been already withdrawn from Longstreet's right to the Warrenton pike, and, together with Hood and Kemper, was pressing down upon Pope's left to crush it back with the last fierce charge of the day, forcing the battle until 9 o'clock that night. Where was Porter then? What was he doing? And only echo answers, where! How did he receive this order to attack? Reclining upon the ground back of Bethlehem church, 2⅔ miles from the front of his column. Sykes was with him, the commander of the regular division, the finest division in the Army. Did he inform Sykes that he was ordered to attack? Not at all. Did he direct him to prepare his division to advance? Did he cause the assembly to be sounded? Did he do anything to indicate that he intended to attempt to obey the order?

General Sykes, before the court-martial, testified as follows (page 178):

Q. Do you know the officer who on the 29th of August bore to General Porter the order of which you have spoken?

A. I do not.

Q. Do you know whether you saw him when he first arrived, or was it on the second arrival?

A. I think it was on his first arrival. General Porter and I were seated together at the time.

Q. Was there any action taken or any order issued immediately on the receipt of the message which that officer bore?

A. I think that some aids-de-camp of General Porter were sent out. I am not positive on that point; but I think Captain Monteith was sent out.

Q. Did General Porter make known to you the character of that order?

A. He did not.

Q. Did he read it in your presence?

A. Not that I know of.

Q. Did you see any order delivered to him by this messenger?

A. I saw a communication delivered to him. I do not know whether it was this order or not.

Q. How long did you remain with General Porter on that occasion after the receipt of this order?

A. I continued with him from that time all night.

Q. You had then, as I understand you to say, no knowledge that a positive order had been given by General Pope on that afternoon for General Porter to attack the enemy on the right flank?

A. I had no such knowledge.

Porter rides to the front, and that is the end of it. "It was quite dark." Yes; it was very dark then in more senses than one. He was justly convicted of disobedience to the 4.30 order to attack.

Next came the following peremptory order, which shows how Pope regarded Porter's conduct:

HEADQUARTERS ARMY OF VIRGINIA,
In the Field, near Bull Run, August 29, 1862—8.50 p. m.

Maj. Gen. F. J. PORTER:

GENERAL: Immediately upon receipt of this order, the precise hour of receiving which you will acknowledge, you will march your command to the field of battle of to-day and report to me in person for orders. *You are to understand that you are expected to comply strictly with this order, and to be present on the field within three hours after its reception, or after daybreak to-morrow morning.*

JOHN POPE,
Major-General, Commanding.

(Received August 30, 3.30 a. m.)

The tone of this order is such as to be insulting in the higest degree to a faithful and subordinate officer.

He might as well have said in so many words, "You have been insubordinate; now you must obey!"

We know that before sending this order Pope had been inclined to order the arrest of Porter for his failure to attack, but had been dissuaded. "What will you say of the 30th," I have been asked. On the 30th Porter was under the immediate eye of Pope. He was stung, evidently, by the order, its tone of reprimand and distrust. And that day he had no choice but fight, and the old Fifth Corps fought as it always fought when it had a chance, with heroic valor. But the desperate valor with which that noble corps fought on the 30th can have nothing to do with the conduct of its commander on the 27th, 28th, and 29th of August.

Pity that so much sacrifice should have been required and so much precious blood wasted to repair the insubordination of the day before.

Such were the events which gave rise to

THE COURT-MARTIAL

and dismissal of General Porter.

That court convened on the 27th of November, 1862. It sat for forty-five days. It was the most elaborate military trial the country ever witnessed.

The court itself was composed of distinguished officers. The following was the detail for the court:

Maj. Gen. D. Hunter, United States Volunteers.
Maj. Gen. E. A. Hitchcock, United States Volunteers.
Brig. Gen. Rufus King, United States Volunteers.
Brig. Gen. B. M. Prentiss, United States Volunteers.
Brig. Gen. James B. Ricketts, United States Volunteers.
Brig. Gen. Silas Casey, United States Volunteers.
Brig. Gen. James A. Garfield, United States Volunteers.
Brig. Gen. N. B. Buford, United States Volunteers.
Bvt. Brig. Gen. W. W. Morris, United States Army.
Col. J. Holt, Judge-Advocate-General, United State Army, judge-advocate and recorder of the court.

On the 10th day of January, 1863, the court rendered its verdict. It found him guilty of three specifications under each of two charges. The merciful sentence was that he should be cashiered. On the 13th the findings were transmitted to the Secretary of War to be laid before President Lincoln. On the 19th the review of the Judge-Advocate-General was laid before the President. On the 21st the President "approved" and confirmed the sentence and carried it into execution. That should have been final. In any other government it would have been final.

Of the thousands of officers and soldiers who have been condemned by courts-martial this case alone is selected for a legislative acquittal—to be legislated into innocence by act of Congress.

However Porter may have lacked in energy on the 27th, 28th, and 29th of August, 1862, he has not lacked in energy since in his efforts to secure the reversal of the verdict of the court; immediately commenced his appeals for a rehearing:

1. Appeal to Grant as Secretary of War, 1866.
2. Appeal to Grant as General, in 1867.
3. Appeal to Grant as President, in 1869.
4. Appeal to Grant as President, in 1874.
5. Appeal to President Hayes, in 1878.

ORDER FOR THE SCHOFIELD BOARD.

Three military gentlemen were invited to compile statements, "that the President may be informed of the facts." It was not a court-martial; not a court of inquiry.

As to the want of power of this board see minority report, page 3:

Not one sentence of the so-called testimony taken before the Schofield board could ever be used as evidence before any court of law or equity in the land. That board had no legal existence; they were bound by no oath of office. The hearing was *ex parte;* there was no process of subpœna for witnesses; no fund to pay their expenses; no person officially charged with the duty of supporting the verdict of the court. No lawful oath was or could be administered to witnesses; no penalty could be imposed for false swearing.

The board perfectly understood this. On page 5 of the proceedings of the board, the president of the board says:

"There is one other matter in regard to which the board would like to hear what counsel have to say; that is in regard to receiving testimony in a case like this, this being *a board having no organization under the law;* no power to summon witnesses or to administer oaths."

Mr. Bullett, of counsel for petitioner, said:

"It is true that the board have no power to administer oaths as far as we can ascertain. * * * As a matter of course many persons may be influenced by the fact that this is not a judicial proceeding; hence the question of perjury might not apply."

On page 6 of the proceedings (Ex. Doc. 37, part 2, Forty-sixth Congress, first session, page 68), the recorder says:

"If the board please, I suppose that the administration of an oath, even by an officer competent to administer oaths, would give no increased validity to statements that may be made here, but it might influence *some* in the manner in which they would give their statements. * * * Of course we know that that which is said here is not in any legal sense evidence, but merely statements."

March 19, 1879, the Schofield board made its report; but so deeply grounded was the confidence of the American people in the court that originally tried him and the President who approved its findings that the report made no perceptible change in the popular conviction that Porter had been justly convicted and dismissed.

The defense made before this board was identical with that made before the court-martial.

As the board themselves say in their report:

The recent testimony of confederate officers hardly adds anything to the conclusiveness of that proof, *but rather diminishes its force*, by showing that one division (Anderson's) did not arrive until the next morning; while the information in their possession at that time required the Union officers *to assume that that division as well as the others* had arrived on the 29th.

The report of the board is a most extraordinary one. It not only absolutely acquits Porter, not only finds him perfectly free of all blame or fault, but it exhausts the vocabulary of eulogy and praise to heap the most fulsome panegyric upon him.

If the report of the Schofield board is a correct judgment in the case, then the court-martial was a hideous conspiracy, to which the General-in-Chief, the War Secretary, the Judge-Advocate-General, and the great and tender-hearted Lincoln were all parties, to sacrifice Porter as a scapegoat for the failure of a campaign then already retrieved. It was not until after it became known that General Grant had espoused Porter's cause, and written to President Arthur to that effect, about December 22, 1881, that the people who had never studied the case for themselves, and who depended upon others for their opinions, began to think that the court-martial might have erred in its judgment. So long as Garfield lived Porter remained quiet. But scarcely had the last painful breath departed from his anguish-racked body when Porter commenced his advances upon the Arthur administration. He knew perfectly well the reverence in which the whole Northern people held the great names of Stanton, Garfield, and Lincoln, and the only possible way to counteract the mighty weight of these names was to throw into the opposite scale a name as great as or even greater than these, the name of Grant.

Garfield was but lately dead. His long and terrible suffering and most pathetic death had made all hearts tender. It was a time for effacing all the scars of war. Four times already Porter had appealed to Grant—in 1866 and 1867, when Grant was General and Secretary of War respectively; to these appeals Grant had turned a deaf ear. Once more, in 1869, when Grant was President and Commander-in-Chief of the Army and Navy—when his power, backed by an overwhelming majority in Congress, was almost unlimited—Porter pressed his appeal. We must presume that the President, as he himself has declared, gave it careful attention. Again he declined to take any action. At this time the newly discovered evidence of Lee and Longstreet was laid before the President.

Once more in 1874, while General Grant was still President, Porter made one more appeal, at this time presenting the additional evidence of Hood, Wilcox, Early, Owens, and Robertson, covering substantially all the ground covered by the board of review, yet without effect.

It was at this time that General Pope wrote to President Grant, among other things saying:

As I do not wish even to *seem* to consent to any additional misconception concerning me or my action in this case, I beg (if you have not already done so) that you will yourself, Mr. President, examine as fully into the question as you think justice or mercy demands.

To this, under date of May 9, 1874, General Grant replied as follows:

* * * You are under the apprehension *that I had not fully examined the case.* * * * I read during the trial the evidence and the final findings of the court, looking upon the whole trial as one of great importance, and particulary so to the Army and Navy. When General Porter's subsequent defense was published *I received a copy of it and read it with care and attention*, determined *if he had been wronged and I could right* him I would do so. My conclusion was that *no new facts* were developed that could be fairly considered, and that it was of *doubtful legality whether by mere authority of the Executive a rehearing could be given.*

Yours, truly,

U. S. GRANT.

General JOHN POPE,
United States Army.

(Volume 3, board proceedings, page 1094.)

President Grant's term of office expired March 4, 1877.

March 9, 1878, General Porter made an appeal to President Hayes. The result was that on the 12th of April the order was issued convening the "Schofield board," consisting of General J. M. Schofield, General A. H. Terry, and Col. George W. Getty: certainly not more distinguished officers than composed the court-martial.

They were appointed by the President on his own motion, without any authority of law.

On March 19, 1879, the board made its report. It was an astonishing document—elaborate, ingenious, the thoroughly partisan plea of an advocate rather than the impartial and candid summing of a judge.

Of all the able and accomplished attorneys who have been employed and paid by Porter in this case, not one has ever made a plea so extravagant, so partisan, so one-sided.

But the great mass of the people, as I have already said, continued to believe that Porter was righteously stripped of the dignities and honors which his country had bestowed upon him. But when, near the beginning of 1882, it became known that our greatest soldier, he who had been our "first in war and first in peace," had brought his powerful advocacy to Porter's cause, many who had neither the time nor the means of examining for themselves yielded their long-settled convictions.

We now find attached to and made a part of the majority report in this case a letter written by General Grant under date of November 23, 1882, directed to General Porter, in which he exonerates him from all blame. This letter being thus made a part and parcel of the majority report, it becomes pertinent and important, as we honor the names of Lincoln and Garfield equally with that of Grant, that we should understand the reason and the basis of this great change—for the opinion of no man of this generation is entitled to more careful consideration and more profound respect at our hands than the opinion of General Grant.

But when we further consider that for nineteen years Grant himself believed Porter guilty as charged, and that too after being four times appealed to, and after reading Porter's defense "with care and attention," and when we find in the letter embodied in the majority report the reasons alleged for his change of belief, it behooves us to examine those reasons with great care.

No man's opinion is worth more than his reasons are worth. And this is true of the greatest as well as of the humblest. No man is equally great in all directions, and we have been sadly reminded of this truth since the last argument of this cause. I am convinced that this change in General Grant's expressed opinion was due to errors and influences easily traced.

I hold in my hand a pamphlet entitled, "General Grant's Unpublished Correspondence in the Case of General Fitz-John Porter." This pamphlet presumably and unquestionably has been printed since the death of General Grant by the authority of Porter himself. It embraces a correspondence extending from September, 1866, to July, 1884, and covers the four rejected appeals of 1866, 1867, 1869, and 1874. During all this long period and down to December, 1881, General Grant firmly believed Porter to be guilty. If he had continued to believe the facts to be as he had previously understood them, he would have continued to believe him guilty to the day of his death. Were those facts as he had understood them or were they not? These nineteen years of firm belief of the great general should not go for nothing, especially when during most of this time he was under official responsibility in the matter.

These letters are an exceedingly valuable contribution to the literature of the case. By their light we are able to understand, I think, in what manner and by what process and by what extent of actual study the change was wrought. The first of these letters, which are significant, is that on page 7, from Porter to Grant.

NEW YORK, *September* 17, 1881.

DEAR GENERAL: *I have been told that you have entertained and sometimes expressed opinions reflecting upon the integrity of my military acts while in the Army.* While I have always been unwilling to believe these reports, I can not help taking them to heart, as I am willing to acknowledge that it would be a matter of wonder if you did not entertain opinions adverse to me, considering the light under which you may have expressed them. * * *

Believe me, very respectfully yours,

F. J. PORTER.

General U. S. GRANT, *Long Branch, N. J.*

To which General Grant replied:

NEW YORK, *September* 27, 1881.

DEAR GENERAL: Your letter of the 17th of September was handed me at Long Branch the *day after the death of the President.* Since that time I have had no opportunity of seeing you, and hence have deferred writing until this time. For a few days I will be so busily employed that I am not able now to appoint a time for the conference which you desire to have with me, but as soon as I can fix a day I will take great pleasure in doing so, and will hear what you have to say in regard to the matter alluded to in your letter, and will endeavor to listen without prejudice, and if convinced that I am *wrong* in former opinions entertained and, possibly, expressed, I would be willing to correct them.

Very truly, yours,

U. S. GRANT.

General F. J. PORTER, 119 *Liberty Street, New York.*

This fixes the fact that up to September 27, 1881, three years after the Schofield board, General Grant had not changed his opinion.

He writes again under date—

New York, *October* 31, 1881.

Dear General: Since my letter to you I have been so busy with correspondence and callers each day that I have not been able to designate a particular time to see you.

If you will call any day, however, at my office, 90 Broadway, about 11 o'clock, I will give you the interview desired, and will keep persons from coming in my office during the time you are with me.

Very truly, yours,

U. S. GRANT.

General F. J. Porter.

Up to October 31 he had no time even for an interview. Nothing had occurred to change his mind.

Congress was about to meet. Porter was anxious to have General Grant's decision at an early day, as upon it depended whether his renewed appeal should be made through the President or direct to Congress. He therefore sent the following note:

New York, *December* 1, 1881.

General: I would be glad of an interview with you to-day, if agreeable, or to-morrow, if more convenient to you.

Yours, truly,

F. J. PORTER.

General U. S. Grant.

This note was returned, indorsed as follows (December 1, 1881):

I will be glad to see you at any time you may call, but *your papers I carried to my house* to go over carefully, but as to yet I have had company every evening at the house—the only time I am there—*so I have not yet examined them sufficiently to say anything.* I think I can safely say, however, that *you will not meet with opposition from me in obtaining relief from the odium of your sentence.* After *examining the papers* before me—which I will do within a few days, if I have to shut myself up for the purpose—if my judgment convinces me that you have been wronged, I will say so.

U. S. GRANT.

The interview did not take place, Porter preferring to wait till the general had formed his convictions.

This is the language of Porter's pamphlet.

From this letter it will be observed that General Grant had been so occupied that he had been able to give little or no attention to the papers sent him by Porter. Yet his mind, by some means, has reached a point where he is able to say, "I think I can safely say, however, that you will not meet with opposition from me in obtaining relief," &c.

Before this, in chronological order, should come in two letters which for some occult reason have been taken out of their proper order and placed at the end of the pamphlet. They are important as showing what new documents, what new evidence were furnished General Grant for his information.

The first one is dated four days after General Grant's letter of October 31, when Grant had not had time to examine the papers, and is as follows:

New York, *November* 4, 1881.

Dear General: If, after you have read the report of the board and my letter to General Cox, you should need any further light or information or proof to sustain anything put forth by the board or by me, I shall be very glad to give it. Yesterday I saw plainly that your impressions of the facts in the case were incorrect, and I am anxious that you should see the facts in their true light, and the more so as the matter was once in your hands to act upon, but you did not act upon, I presume, because of such impressions as you expressed yesterday.

I will try to present my case to you clearly and dispassionately, believing that you will receive them as dispassionately and free from prejudice, and with as great a desire to undo any wrong unintentionally done as you would have done right in the first case.

My statement sent to you yesterday was mainly written in 1863, added to as time sustained my views by proofs, and but slightly altered by my counsel for presentation to the Schofield board. The foot-notes were added after the adjournment of the board, and when the Senate was printing the proceedings. * * *

Respectfully yours,

F. J. PORTER.

From this we see that up to "yesterday" (November 3) Grant's "impressions of the facts of the case were incorrect." We also see the subtle appeal to his feelings, because "the matter was once in your hands to act upon, but you did not act." It also shows the papers furnished by Porter. They were "the report of the board," "my letter to General Cox," "my statement sent you yesterday," "mainly written in 1863," "the foot-notes added after the adjournment of the board."

The following comes immediately after the last, without date, and seems to be a postscript to it. (Date would be November 4.)

GENERAL U. S. GRANT: I inclose a copy of *my defense before the court-martial*, written by Mr. Eames and prepared from the imperfect evidence of fact on the record, but at that time—with the obstacles thrown in the way of getting evidence—all the evidence I could bring forward. *It is substantially the same argument as now made.*

Yours, respectfully,

F. J. PORTER.

So that by Porter's own admission the case made to General Grant was "substantially the same" that was made before the court-martial in 1863. No more, no less, in substance.

We may also see what he did not have:

NEW YORK, *December* 23, 1881.

DEAR SIR: * * * I will be pleased if you will send me a copy of the proceedings of the board, as published by the Senate.

Truly yours,

U. S. GRANT.

General F. J. PORTER, *New York.*

It would seem that he did not have the proceedings of the board, which contained the evidence in the case.

The next letter (but dated the day before) is to President Arthur, and shows the amount of time given to the study of the case:

NEW YORK, *December* 22, 1881.

DEAR SIR: At the request of General Fitz-John Porter I have recently reviewed his trial and the testimony furnished before the Schofield court of inquiry, held in 1879, giving to the subject three full days of careful reading and consideration, and much thought in the intervening time. The reading of the whole of this record has thoroughly convinced me that for these nineteen years I have been doing a gallant and efficient soldier a very great injustice in thought, and sometimes in speech.

* * * * * * *

I am, very truly, yours,

U. S. GRANT.

The PRESIDENT, *Washington, D. C.*

I desire to make only one comment upon this correspondence.

It is admitted that the argument made to Grant in 1881 was substantially the same as made to Garfield as a member of the court, who was solemnly sworn to try the case "without fear, favor, affection, or hope of reward," in 1863.

Grant gave to the case three days—at least all the time he could give to it in "three full days."

Garfield give to it forty-five full days.

Grant had only one side presented to him.

Garfield had both sides, on the facts, but argument only for the defense.

Garfield had all the living witnesses before him. He looked into their eyes, witnessed their bearing, heard the tones of their voice, saw them under the fire of cross-examination.

Grant had none of these.

Garfield added to the honor and chivalry of the soldier the intellectual discipline, the logical mind, the keen discrimination of the trained lawyer.

Grant, with that kind-hearted magnanimity which in his later years made him desire the good-will of every heart that had in any way been wounded by the unhappy strife of war, and feeling that when he had this man absolutely in his hands he had been wholly deaf to his appeal, was unquestionably disposed to place the most optimistic construction upon every act and apparent neglect of duty.

Grant had before him everything that would exculpate, nothing that would condemn.

But in the letter which forms a part of the majority report General Grant has given us for himself the reasons for his change of mind. This letter, as embodied in the report, bears date November 3, 1883. In the pamphlet of General Porter it is dated November 23. I shall incorporate only a portion of it in my remarks:

NEW YORK, *November* 3, 1883.

DEAR GENERAL: As there is some discussion as to the probable reasons for my change of mind in regard to your case, now pending before the people of the United States, I deem it proper *that I should give them myself.*

In the first place, I never believed you to be a traitor, as many affected to believe. I thought I knew you too well to believe for one moment that you would accept the pay, rank, and command you held for the purpose of betraying the cause you were professing to serve. Then, too, your services had been too conspicuous as a staff officer at the beginning of the war and as commander of troops later, to support such a theory for a moment.

But *I did believe that General Pope was so odious to some of the officers in the East that a cordial support was not given him by them.* I was disposed, too, to accept the verdict of a court-martial composed as the one which tried you was. Some of the members of that court I knew personally, and had great confidence in their judgment and justice. I supposed you had shared in this feeling toward Pope, and while not more guilty than others, you were unfortunate in being placed in a position where specifications could be made showing this hostility.

After the close of the war, when I was requested to read your new defense, I read it with the feeling above described. At the same time I read the other side as prepared—or furnished—by General Pope. This gave maps showing the positions of the two armies substantially as shown by the first of the diagrams presented by Mr. Lord, of San Francisco, from whom I copied the article in your case, and did not indicate the presence of any other force than Jackson's. *Then, too, it appeared that you had actually received an order at about* 5 *or* 5.30 *in the afternoon of August* 29 *to attack the enemy's flank, and that, too, at a time when a fierce battle was raging in the front.*

I was first shaken in my views, however, when such a man as General Terry—who unites the lawyer with the soldier—a man of high character and ability, and who had believed as I had and possibly worse, after many weeks of investigation, should entirely vindicate you and be sustained, too, by men of the known ability of his colleagues on the board. Until in 1881, when I re-examined for myself, my belief was that, [1] on the 29th of August, 1862, a great battle was fought between General Pope, commanding the Union forces, and General Jackson, commanding the confederate forces; [2] that you, with a corps of twelve or more thousand men, stood in a position across the right flank of Jackson, and where you could easily get into his rear; [3] that you received an order to do so about 5 or 5.30 o'clock, which you refused to obey because of clouds of dust in your front, which you contended indicated an enemy in superior force to you; [4] that you allowed Pope to get beaten while you stood idly looking on without raising an arm to help him. With this understanding, and without a doubt as to the correctness of it, I condemned you.

Now, on a full investigation of the facts, *I find that the battle was fought on the 30th of August;* that your corps, commanded directly by you in person, lost a greater percentage than any other corps engaged; that the 4.30 order of the day before did not reach you until night-fall; that your immediate superior had cautioned you early in the day that you were too far out to the front then; that General Pope had cautioned you against bringing on an engagement except under such circumstances as he described, and that in any event you must be prepared to fall back behind Bull Run that night, where it would be necessary for you to be to receive supplies; *that from 11 o'clock of the 29th you were confronted by a force of twice your own number, of whose presence you had positive proof, while General Pope did not know of it.*

* * * * * * *

Your knowledge of this fact, as well as of the fact that you had another force, quite double yours, in addition in your front, would have been sufficient justification for your not attacking, even if the order had been received in time. Of course this would not apply if a battle had been raging between Jackson and Pope. At the hour you received the order all was quiet.

* * * * * * *

Faithfully yours,

U. S. GRANT.

General F. J. PORTER.

General Grant says he condemned Porter because he believed four things:

1. That a great battle was fought on the 29th of August, 1862.
2. That Porter stood with a corps of twelve thousand or more men across the enemy's right flank.
3. That he received an order to attack which he failed to obey.
4. That he allowed Pope to get beaten while he stood idly looking on.

Believing this, he for nineteen years condemned Porter.

If these suppositions were correct Grant would still have condemned him.

1. I think that I have already shown that Porter did stand "with a corps of twelve thousand or more men" across the enemy's right flank.
2. That he received an order to attack which he could have obeyed, and ought to have obeyed, but did not obey.
3. That he allowed Pope to get beaten, and that too on the portion of the battlefield nearest Porter's troops, while he stood (or rather lay) idly looking on.

But he says: "I find that the battle was fought on the 30th of August."

Again he says: "Of course this would not apply if a battle had been raging between Jackson and Pope."

So that now the issue is distinctly raised, both by the letter of General Grant and by the report of the Schofield board, whether there was

A BATTLE ON AUGUST 29 AT GROVETON.

General Grant says in his letter that "until 1881 * * * my belief was that on the 29th of August, 1862, a great battle was fought." Now, here is an amazing thing, that for nineteen years the General of the Army should have believed that a great battle was fought, when, in point of fact, no battle was fought. And this great battle is made to disappear from history in the interest of the relief of Fitz-John Porter. [Applause.]

General Grant says in the majority report: "Of course this would not apply if a battle had been raging." Hence the battle must not rage! One of the great battles of the war must be wiped out to afford an excuse for Porter's not obeying a peremptory order to attack.

It appears to me, Mr. Chairman, that it is about time that this great historical question were settled and determined.

Since the last discussion of this bill in this House the publication of the Official Record of the War of the Rebellion has covered the epoch from August 27 to September 30, and we are permitted access to the official reports of the officers who commanded the troops on both sides upon August 29.

I propose that, so far as in me lies, this question shall be settled, that it shall be settled now and settled forever. And if any gentleman of this House shall vote for this bill—shall vote that Porter was not under obligation to obey an imperative order to attack—it shall not be upon the false and flimsy ground that there was no battle upon the 29th of August.

Before entering upon a discussion of the facts, Mr. Chairman, I desire to call attention to some general features of battles.

The greatness of a battle depends upon several things:

1. The magnitude of the forces engaged;
2. The duration of the conflict;
3. The energy or fierceness of the collision;
4. The losses ot life and force; and
5. The decisive character of the result.

There are battles, and then there are *battles*. There are battles that are to a finish, and then there are battles that are not to a finish. The battle of August 29 was of the latter class; so were the first two days at Gettysburg, and the first day at Shiloh. No battle lasts, as a rule, with continuous fury along the whole line all day long. That would not be possible; flesh and blood could not stand it.

In the late war it was my lot to share in some of the larger engagements, including Fredericksburg, Vicksburg, Wilderness, Spottsylvania, and Petersburg. I never knew a battle that was not made up of a series of conflicts, at different hours, and on different parts of the line with intervals between.

Perhaps the most decisive battle yet fought upon this continent was the third day at Gettysburg, yet the first signal gun was fired after 1 o'clock, and after an artillery duel of about an hour the infantry advanced to the assault.

In two hours the battle was practically over.

I know there are soldiers here who were in that battle. Do not understand me to say that there was not fighting in the morning; that there was not fighting after Pickett's division was repulsed. There was fighting all day, but the decisive battle was between 1 and 3 o'clock.

At Fredericksburg the battle commenced in the early morning by Franklin's attack on the left, was followed by Hooker on the extreme right and Sumner in the center, and was renewed at wide intervals of time and space, until the final assault by Humphrey's division was made after dark.

The same is true of the battle of the Wilderness. I think it can be said that at no one time were all the forces on either side engaged.

I propose to apply these usual and recognized tests to the action of the 29th of August to determine whether a battle, in the proper sense of that word, was fought on that day. The sources of information upon which I shall rely are the official reports of the commanding officers on either side, in most cases made immediately or very soon thereafter. These reports, with the possible exception of General Pope's, were made without any reference to Porter's case.

ORGANIZATION OF POPE'S ARMY.

	Divisions.
1. Sigel's corps	Schenck. Schurz. Milroy.
2. Heintzelman's corps	Hooker. Kearny.
3. McDowell's corps	King. Reynolds. Ricketts.
4. Reno's corps	Stevens.
5. Porter's corps	Sykes. Morell. Piatt's brigade.

All the following extracts except the first are from the official reports embraced in part 2, volume 12, War of the Rebellion, published by the War Department, and relate exclusively to the battle of the 29th, unless otherwise shown upon their face.

HEADQUARTERS, FIELD OF BATTLE,
Near Groveton, Va.—5 a. m., August 30, 1862.

Maj. Gen. H. W. HALLECK,
General-in-Chief, United States Army:

We fought a terrific battle here yesterday with the combined forces of the enemy, which lasted with continuous fury from daylight until after dark. * * *
The enemy is still in our front, but badly used up. We lost not less than eight thousand men killed and wounded. * * *

JOHN POPE, *Major-General.*

(Page 388, board proceedings.)

[Report of Maj. Gen. John Pope, U. S. Army, of the operations of the Army of Virginia June 26–September 2, with orders and correspondence.]

HEADQUARTERS ARMY OF VIRGINIA, *September* 3, 1862.

* * * * * * *

Heintzelman marched early from Centreville toward Gainesville, closely followed by Reno.

Meantime, shortly after daylight, Sigel, and Reynolds's division of McDowell's corps, had become engaged with the enemy, who was brought to a stand, and he was soon joined by Heintzelman and Reno, and the whole line became actively engaged. Porter marched as directed, followed by King's division, which was by this time joined by Ricketts's division, which had been forced back from Thoroughfare Gap by the heavy forces of the enemy advancing to support Jackson.

As soon as I found that the enemy had been brought to a halt and was being vigorously attacked along Warrenton turnpike I sent orders to McDowell to advance rapidly on our left and attack the enemy on his flank, extending his right to meet Reynolds's left, and to Fitz-John Porter to keep the right well closed on McDowell's left and to attack the enemy in flank and rear while he was pushed in front. This would have made the line of battle of McDowell and Porter at right angles to that of the other forces engaged. The action raged furiously all day, McDowell, although previously in rear of Porter, bringing his whole corps on the field in the afternoon and taking a conspicuous part in that day's operations.

To my surprise and disappointment I received late in the afternoon from Porter a note saying that his advance had met the enemy on the flank in some force, and that he was retiring upon Manassas Junction, without attacking the enemy or coming to the assistance of our other forces, although they were engaged in a furious action only 2 miles distant and in full hearing of him. A portion of his force fell back toward Manassas, and he remained, as he afterward informed me, where he was, looking at the enemy during the whole of the afternoon of Friday and part of Friday night passing down in plain view to re-enforce the troops under Jackson without an effort to prevent it or to assist us. One, at least, of his brigades, under General Griffin, got around to Centreville and remained there during the whole of the next day's battle without coming on the field, though in full view of it, while General Griffin himself spent the day in making ill-natured strictures upon the general commanding [see paper marked D] the action in the presence of a promiscuous assemblage.

Darkness closed the action on Friday, the enemy being driven back from his position by Heintzelman's corps and Reno, concluded by a furious attack along the turnpike by King's division, of McDowell's corps, leaving his dead and wounded on the field.

* * * * * * *

I have much to say and to report to you concerning the conduct of certain officers and their commands during these operations, which I will postpone for the present. There is no doubt in the mind of any man here that the battle of Groveton would have been a decisive and complete victory on the first day had General Porter advanced as I directed him. Why he did not is yet unexplained. The whole of the heavy re-enforcements which attacked us on Saturday passed down the road from Gainesville during the whole afternoon and night of Friday, while General Porter remained in full sight of them, on their flank, between Manassas Junction and Gainesville, although he had my positive written order to attack them in flank while I was urging the battle in front. He made no attack whatever, but retired a portion of his command, at least, to Manassas, which was not near enough the next day to take any part in the action.

[Report of Maj Gen. Franz Sigel, United States Army, commanding First Corps, Army of Virginia, of operations along the Rappahannock and the battles of Groveton and Bull Run.]

HEADQUARTERS FIRST CORPS, ARMY OF VIRGINIA,
Near Fort De Kalb, Va., September 16, 1862.

* * * * * * *

On the night of August 28, when the First Corps was encamped on the heights south of Young's Branch, near Bull Run, I received orders to "attack the enemy vigorously" the next morning. I accordingly made the necessary preparations at night and formed in order of battle at daybreak, having ascertained that the enemy was in considerable force beyond Young's Branch, in sight of the hills we occupied. His left wing rested on Catharpin Creek, front toward Centreville; with his center he occupied a long stretch of woods parallel with the Sudley Springs-New Market road, and his right was posted on the hills on both sides of the Centreville-Gainesville road. I therefore directed General Schurz to deploy his division on the right of Gainesville road, and by a change of direction to the left to come into position parallel with the Sudley Springs road. General Milroy, with his brigade and one battery, was directed to form the center, and to take possession of an elevation in front of the so-called "stone house," at the junction of the Gainesville and Sudley Springs roads. General Schenck, with his division, forming our left, was ordered to advance quickly to an adjoining range of hills, and to plant his batteries on these hills at an excellent range from the enemy's position.

In this order our whole line advanced from point to point, taking advantage of the ground before us, until our whole line was involved in a most vehement artillery and infantry contest. In the course of about four hours, from 6.30 to 10.30 o'clock in the morning, our whole infantry force and nearly all our batteries were engaged with the enemy, Generals Milroy and Schurz advancing 1 mile and General Schenck 2 miles from their original positions.

At this time (10.30 o'clock) the enemy threw forward large masses of infantry against our right, but was resisted firmly and driven back three times by the troops of Generals Milroy and Schurz. To assist these troops so hard pressed by overpowering numbers, exhausted by fatigue, and weakened by losses, I ordered one battery of reserve to take position on their left, and posted two pieces of artillery under Lieutenant Blume, of Schirmer's battery, supported by the Forty-first New York Volunteer Infantry, beyond their line and opposite the right flank of the enemy, who was advancing in the woods. These pieces opened fire with canister most effectively and checked the enemy's advance on that point. I now directed General Schenck to draw his lines nearer to us and to attack the enemy's right flank and rear by a change of front to the right, thereby assisting our troops in the center. This movement could not be executed by General Schenck with his whole division, as he became briskly engaged with the enemy, who tried to turn our extreme left.

At this critical moment, when the enemy had almost outflanked us on both wings, and was preparing a new attack against our center, Major-General Kearny arrived on the field of battle, and deployed by Sudley Springs road on our right, while General Reno's troops came to our support by the Gainesville turnpike. With the consent of General Reno I directed two regiments and one battery, under Brigadier-General Stevens, to take position on the right of General Schenck—the battery on an eminence in front and center of our line, where it did excellent work during the rest of the day, and where it relieved Captain

Dilger's battery, which had held this position the whole morning. Three regiments were posted between General Milroy and General Schenck, and two others, with two mountain howitzers, were sent to the assistance of General Schurz. Scarcely were these troops in position when the contest began with renewed vigor and vehemence, the enemy attacking furiously along our whole line, from the extreme right to the extreme left.

At 2 o'clock in the afternoon General Hooker's troops arrived on the field of battle, and were immediately ordered forward by their noble commander to participate in the battle. One brigade, under Colonel Carr, received orders, by my request, to relieve the regiments of General Schurz's division, which had maintained their ground against repeated attacks, but were now worn out and nearly without ammunition. Other regiments were sent forward to relieve Brigadier-General Milroy, whose brigade had valiantly disputed the ground against greatly superior numbers for eight hours.

* * * * * * *

During two hours, from 4 to 6 p. m., strong cannonading and musketry continued on our center and right, where General Kearny made a successful effort against the extreme left of the enemy's lines.

At 6.15 o'clock Brigadier-General King's division of Major-General McDowell's corps arrived behind our front, and advanced on the Gainesville turnpike. I do not know the real result of this movement, but from the weakness of the enemy's cannonade and the gradually decreasing musketry in the direction of General Kearny's attack, I received the impression that the enemy's resistance was broken, and that victory was on our side; and so it was. We had won the field of battle, and our army rested near the dead and wounded who had so gloriously defended the good cause of this country. (Pages 266, 267.)

[Report of Brig. Gen. R. C. Schenck, commanding first division.]

WASHINGTON, D. C., *September* 17, 1862.

* * * * * * *

On Friday morning early the engagement was commenced by General Milroy on our right, in which we soon took part, and a rapid artillery fire ensued from both sides. * * * Milroy in the mean while had deployed to the right of the road, and soon became engaged with the enemy. Our division was advanced until we reached the edge of the woods and halted. In front of us was an open space (which also extended to the right of the road and to our right) beyond which was another wood. We remained here nearly an hour, the firing in the meanwhile becoming heavy on the right. The enemy had a battery very advantageously placed on a high ridge behind the woods in front of Milroy, on the right of the road. It was admirably served and entirely concealed. Our position becoming known, their fire was directed toward us. The general determined, therefore, to advance, and so pushed on across the open space in front and took position in the woods beyond. We here discovered that we were on the battle-ground of the night before, and found the hospital of Gibbon's brigade, who had engaged the enemy. The battery of the enemy still continued. We had no artillery. De Beck's and Schirmer's ammunition having given out, and Buell's battery, which had reported, after a hot contest with the enemy (who had every advantage in position and range), was compelled to retire.

It was now determined to flank the battery and capture it, and for this purpose General Schenck ordered one of his aids to reconnoiter the position. Before he returned, however, we were requested by General Milroy to assist him, as he was very heavily pressed. General Stahel was immediately ordered to proceed with his brigade to Milroy's support. It was about this time (1 or 2 o'clock) that a line of skirmishers were observed approaching us from the rear. They proved to be of General Reynolds's division. We communicated with General Reynolds at once, who took his position on our left, and at General Schenck's suggestion he sent a battery to our right in the woods for the purpose of flanking the enemy's. They secured a position, and were engaged with him about an hour, but with what result we were not informed. General Reynolds now sent us word that he had discovered the enemy bearing down upon his left in heavy columns, and that he intended to fall back to the first woods behind the cleared space, and had already put his troops in motion. We therefore accommodated ourselves to his movement. (Page 280.)

[Report of Brig. Gen. Carl Schurz, United States Army, commanding Third Division, of the battles of Groveton and Bull Run.]

HEADQUARTERS THIRD DIVISION,
Camp near Minor's Hill, September 15, 1862.

GENERAL: I have the honor to submit the following report concerning the part taken by the division under my command in the battles of the 29th and 30th of August:

On the evening of the 28th of August my division was encamped south of the turnpike leading from Centreville to Gainesville, near Mrs. Henry's farm. On the 29th, a little after 5 o'clock a. m., you ordered me to cross the turnpike, to deploy my division north of it, and to attack the forces of the enemy supposed to be concealed in the woods immediately in my front, my division forming the right wing of your army corps. * * * I pushed my left wing rapidly forward into the long stretch of woods before me, and found myself obliged to extend my line considerably in order to establish the connection with General Milroy, which, however, was soon effected.

Hardly had this been done when the fire commenced near the point where General Milroy's right touched my left. I placed the battery of the second brigade upon an elevation of ground, about 600 or 700 yards behind the point where that brigade had entered the woods a little to the left, so as to protect the retreat of the regiments composing the left wing, in case they should be forced to fall back. The battery of the first brigade remained for the same purpose on high ground behind the woods in which Colonel Schimmelfennig was engaged, covering my right. When the fire of the skirmishers had been going on a little while two prisoners were brought to me, sent by Colonel Schimmelfennig, who stated that there was a very large force of the enemy (Ewell's and Jackson's divisions) immediately in my front, and about the same time one of Colonel Schimmelfennig's aides informed me that heavy columns of troops were seen moving on my right flank, and that it could not be distinguished whether they were Union troops or rebels. I then withdrew the reserve regiment of the second brigade (the Fifty-fourth New York) from the woods, so as to have it at my disposal in an emergency, and ordered Colonel Schimmelfennig to form one of his regiments front toward the right and to send out skirmishers in that direction, so as to ascertain the true condition of things there.

Meanwhile the fire in front had extended along the whole line and become very lively, my regiments pushing the enemy vigorously before them about one-half mile. The discharges of musketry increased in rapidity and volume as we advanced, and it soon became evident that the enemy was throwing heavy masses against us. About that time General Steinwehr brought the Twenty-ninth New York, under Colonel Soest, to my support, and formed it in line of battle on the edge of the roads behind a fence. I then received information that the columns which had appeared on my right, and which really seemed to have belonged to the enemy, had disappeared again in the woods without making any demonstration, and also that General Kearny's troops were coming up in my rear. Thus reassured about the safety of my right, and expecting more serious business in the center, I sent the Fifty-fourth New York forward again, with the order to fill up the gap between my two brigades occasioned by the extension of my line toward General Milroy's right. The Twenty-ninth New York remained in reserve.

Immediately afterward the enemy began to press my center so severely that it gave way; but we soon rallied it again, and after a sharp contest reoccupied the ground previously taken from the enemy. It was about 10 o'clock a. m. when an officer announced to me that General Kearny had arrived on the battlefield and desired to see me. General Kearny requested me to shorten my front and condense my line by drawing my right nearer to the left, so as to make room for him on the right. I gave my orders to Colonel Schimmelfennig accordingly. A short time afterward I discovered that two small regiments sent to my support had slipped in between my two brigades, and were occupying part of my line in the woods. General Kearny was just moving up his troops on my right when the enemy made another furious charge upon my center. The two regiments above mentioned, as well as the Fifty-fourth New York, broke and were thrown out of the woods in disorder.

* * * * * * *

The Twenty-ninth New York and the Fifty-fourth New York had just re-entered the woods when one of your aides presented to me for perusal a letter which you had addressed to General Kearny, requesting him to attack at once with his whole force, as the rebel General Longstreet who was expected to re-enforce the enemy during the day had not yet arrived upon the battlefield, and we might hope to gain decisive advantage before his arrival. I then ordered a general advance of my whole line, which was executed with great gallantry, the enemy yielding everywhere before us.

* * * * * * *

Now the whole line advanced with great alacrity, and we succeeded in driving the enemy away from his strong position behind the embankment, which then fell into our hands on my left also.

While this was going on I heard from time to time very heavy firing on my left, where General Milroy stood. The sound of the musketry was swaying forward and backward, indicating that the fight was carried on with alternate success. The connection of my left with General Milroy's right was lost, and I found my left uncovered. However, we succeeded in holding the position of the railroad embankment along my whole front against the repeated attacks of the enemy until about 2 o'clock p. m., when my troops, who had started at 5 o'clock in the morning, mostly without breakfast, had been under fire for eight hours, had been decimated by enormous losses, and had exhausted nearly all their ammunition, were relieved by a number of regiments kindly sent by General Hooker for that purpose. These re-enforcements arrived in my front between 1 and 2 o'clock. According to your order, I withdrew my regiments, one after another, as their places were filled by those of General Hooker. Thus the possession of that portion of the woods which my division had taken and held was in good order delivered to the troops that relieved me. * * * Exhausted and worn down as my men were my division was unable to take part in the action after 2 o'clock p. m., nor was I called upon to do so.

[Report of Brig. Gen. Robert H. Milroy, United States Army, commanding independent brigade, First Corps, Army of Virginia, of operations August 13-31.]

HEADQUARTERS INDEPENDENT BRIGADE,
Near Fort Ethan Allen, Virginia, September 12, 1862.

* * * * * * *

On the following morning (the 29th), at daylight, I was ordered to proceed in search of the rebels, and had not proceeded more than 500 yards when we were greeted by a few straggling shots from the woods in front. We were now at the creek, and I had just sent forward my skirmishers, when I received orders to halt and let the men have breakfast. While they were cooking, myself, accompanied by General Schenck, rode up to the top of an eminence, some 500 yards to the front, to reconnoiter. We had no sooner reached the top than we were greeted by a shower of musket balls from the woods on our right. I immediately ordered up my battery and gave the bushwhackers a few shot and shell, which soon cleared the woods. Soon after I discovered the enemy in great force about three-quarters of a mile in front of us, upon our right of the pike leading from Gainesville to Alexandria. I brought up my two batteries and opened upon them, causing them to fall back. I then moved forward my brigade, with skirmishers deployed, and continued to advance my regiments, the enemy falling back.

General Schenck's division was off to my left and that of General Schurz to my right. After passing a piece of woods I turned to the right, where the rebels had a battery that gave us a great deal of trouble. I brought forward one of my batteries to reply to it, and soon after heard a tremendous fire of small-arms, and knew that General Schurz was hotly engaged to my right in an extensive forest. I sent two of my regiments, the Eighty-second Ohio, Colonel Cantwell, and the Fifth Virginia, Colonel Zeigler, to General Schurz's assistance. They were to attack the enemy's right flank, and I held my other two regiments in reserve for a time.

The two regiments sent to Shurz were soon hotly engaged, the enemy being behind a railroad embankment, which afforded them an excellent breastwork. The railroad had to be approached from the cleared ground on our side through a strip of thick timber from 100 to 500 yards in width. I had intended, with the two regiments held in reserve (the Second and Third Virginia Regiments), to charge the rebel battery, which was but a short distance from us over the top of a hill to our left, but while making my arrangements to do this I observed that my two regiments engaged were being driven back out of the woods by the terrible fire of the rebels.

I then saw the brave Colonels Cantwell and Zeigler struggling to rally their broken regiments on the rear of the forest out of which they had been driven, and sent two of my aids to assist them and assure them of immediate support. They soon rallied their men and charged again and again up to the railroad, but were driven back each time with great loss. I then sent the Second Virginia to their support, directing it to approach the railroad at the point on the left of my other regiments, where the woods ended, but they were met by such a destructive fire from a large rebel force that they were soon thrown into confusion and fell back in disorder. The enemy now came on in overwhelming numbers. General Carl Schurz had been obliged to retire with his two brigades an hour before, and then the whole rebel force was turned against my brigade, and my brave lads were dashed back before the storm of bullets like chaff before the tempest. I then ordered my reserve battery into position a short distance in the rear, and when five guns had got into position one of the wheel horses was shot dead, but I ordered it to unlimber where they were, and the six guns mowed the rebels with grape and canister with fine effect.

My reserved regiment, the Third Virginia, now opened with telling effect. Colonel Cantwell, of the Eighty-second Ohio, was shot through the brain and instantly killed while trying to rally his regiment during the thickest of the fight.

While the storm was raging the fiercest, General Stahel came to me and reported that he had been sent by General Schenck to support me, and inquired where he should place his brigade. I told him on my left, and help support my battery. He then returned to his brigade, and soon after being attacked from another quarter, I did not again see him during the day. I was left wholly unsupported, except by a portion of a Pennsylvania regiment, which I found on the field, and stood by me bravely during the next hour or two. I then rallied my reserved regiment and broken fragments in the woods near my battery, and sent out a strong party of skirmishers to keep the enemy at bay, while another party went forward without arms to get off as many of our dead and wounded as possible. I maintained my ground, skirmishing, and occasionally firing by battalion during the greater part of the afternoon.

Toward evening General Grover came up with his New England brigade. I saw him forming a line to attack the rebel stronghold in the same place I had been all day, and advised him to form line more to the left, and charge bayonets on arriving at the railroad track, which his brigade executed with such telling effect as to drive the rebels in clouds before their bayonets. Meanwhile I had gathered the remnant of my brigade, ready to take advantage of any opportunity to assist him. I soon discovered a large number of rebels fleeing before the left flank of Grover's brigade. They passed over an open space some 500 yards in width in front of my reserved regiment, which I ordered to fire on them, which they did, accelerating their speed and discomfiture so much that I ordered a charge. My regiment immediately dashed out of the woods we were in down across the meadows in front of us after the retreating foe, but before their arriving at the other side of the meadow the retreating column received a heavy support from the railroad below them, and, soon rallying, came surging back, driving before their immense columns Grover's brigade and my handful of men.

An hour before the charge I had sent one of my aids back after a fresh battery—the ammunition of both my batteries having given out—which arriving as our boys were being driven back I immediately ordered them into position and commenced pouring a steady fire of grape and canister into the advancing columns of the enemy. The first discharge discomposed them a little, but the immense surging mass behind pressed them on us. I held on until they were within 100 yards of us, and having but a handful of men to support the battery, ordered it to retire, which was executed with the loss of one gun. I then rallied the shattered remnant of my brigade, which had been rallied by my aids and its officers, and encamped some three-quarters of a mile to the rear.

[Reports of Maj. Gen. Irvin McDowell, United States Army, commanding Third Corps, Army of Virginia, of operations August 7-September 2.]

WASHINGTON, D. C., *November* 6, 1862.

* * * * * * *

Early in the morning of the 29th General Sigel, who had come up the night before from near Manassas, and who was on Reynold's right, made demonstrations against the enemy, who seemed to be on the north of us. I directed Reynolds to support General Sigel on the left in the movements he might make, and then proceeded to join Generals King's and Ricketts's divisions.

At Manassas I found Maj. Gen. Fitz-John Porter's corps coming up, and soon after, in answer partly to a message of mine, I received your order of the 29th from Centreville, addressed jointly to General Porter and myself. In compliance with it, King's and Ricketts's divisions were directed, as soon as they could be placed on the road from Manassas Junction to Gainesville, which runs nearly west, to follow in the rear and close to General Porter's corps. Both these divisions had been on foot night and day for several days past, had marched the most of the night before, and were separated from their baggage and subsistence. They moved forward, however, cheerfully. The column coming to a halt, I rode forward and found General Porter at the head of his corps, on a slight eminence; in front was an open piece of ground, and beyond it the woods skirting the Warrenton road, down which, as we could see from the dust above the trees, the enemy was moving from Gainesville upon Groveton, where the battle was now going on.

Just before reaching General Porter I received a note from General Buford, commanding cavalry brigade, who was on our then left and front, acquainting me with the strength of the enemy, which he had seen as they passed through

Gainesville, then moving down the road. It consisted of seventeen regiments, one battery, and five hundred cavalry. As this was an inferior force to General Porter's, I decided for him to throw himself at once on the enemy's flank, and as the head of my column was some 3 miles back, near the Sudley Springs road, I would move it directly north on that road upon the field where the battle was then at its height.

Generals Seymour and Jackson led their brigades in advance, but notwithstanding all the steadiness and courage of the men they were compelled, by the fire of the enemy's artillery and infantry on their front and left, to resume their former position.

Immediately on my arrival with King's division I directed it to move forward and take place on the left of Reynolds's, then still engaged on the left of Sigel's corps, and some of the brigades went forward to do so, when I received your instructions to order the division over to the north of the turnpike to support the line held by Reno, which had been hotly engaged all day, and the division was recalled and brought back to the Sudley Springs road for this purpose.

One of the brigades—Patrick's—having received an order, as he informed me, direct from your headquarters, to move across the field, became separated from the division, and though he moved at the quickest pace, was not able to rejoin until late that evening.

About the time the division arrived at the crossing of the Sudley Springs and Warrenton turnpike I received word from you that the enemy were falling back, and to send the division right up the turnpike after them. It was now near dusk, and though the men had been on foot since 1 o'clock in the morning they moved forward with the greatest enthusiasm. They were led gallantly up the road by Brigadier-General Hatch, who, trusting to find the enemy in retreat as he was told, and hoping to turn their retreat into a flight, took the men forward, his own and Doubleday's brigades and Gerrish's battery of howitzers, with Patrick's brigade in reserve, with an impetuosity akin to rashness. The attack was severe, both on the enemy and our men.

About the same time an attack was made by Bayard's cavalry, on the left of Hatch, on the enemy south of the road, in which Seymour's squadron suffered severely. These were the finishing strokes of the day, which we could now safely claim as ours. (Pages 337, 338, and 339.)

[Report of Brig. Gen. John P. Hatch, United States Army, commanding first (King's) division, of the battles of Groveton and Bull Run.]

CAMP NEAR FREDERICK, MD., *September* 13, 1862.

CAPTAIN: I have the honor to submit the following report of the movements of the first division, Third Corps, temporarily under my command during parts of the 29th and 30th days of August:

Late on the afternoon of the 29th ultimo I was ordered by General McDowell in person (who was at the time stationed near the stone house on the turnpike from Gainesville to Centreville) to move the division on the Gainesville road in pursuit of the enemy, who, he informed me, were retreating. Gibbon's brigade had been detached to support some batteries. With the three other brigades of the division and Gerrish's battery of howitzers, I proceeded with all the speed possible, hoping, by harassing the enemy's rear, to turn their retreat into a rout.

After marching about three-quarters of a mile the Second Regiment of United States Sharpshooters was deployed to the front as skirmishers, the column continuing up the road in support. The advance almost immediately became warmly engaged on the left of the road. Two howitzers were then placed in position, one on each side of the road, and Doubleday's brigade was deployed to the front, on the left of the road, and moved up to the support of the skirmishers. We were met by a force consisting of three brigades of infantry, one of which was posted in the woods on the left, parallel to and about an eighth of a mile from the road. The two other brigades were drawn up in line of battle, one on each side of the road. These were in turn supported by a large portion of the rebel forces, estimated by a prisoner, who was taken to their rear, at about thirty thousand men, drawn up in successive lines, extending 1¼ miles to the rear. Doubleday's brigade moved to the front under a very heavy fire, which they gallantly sustained; but the firing continuing very heavy, Hatch's brigade, commanded by Colonel Sullivan, was also deployed, and moved to the support of General Doubleday. Patrick's brigade, which had been held in reserve, took up a position on the opposite side of the road, completely commanding it. The struggle, lasting some three-quarters of an hour, was a desperate one, being in many instances a hand-to-hand conflict.

Night had now come on, our loss had been severe, and the enemy occupying a position in the woods on our left which gave them a flank fire upon us, I was forced to give the order for a retreat. The retreat was executed in good order, the attempt of the enemy to follow being defeated by a few well-directed volleys from Patrick's brigade. (Page 367.)

[Report of Brig. Gen. Abner Doubleday.]

NOVEMBER 2, 1862.

* * * * * * *

At 1 a. m. on the 29th the division moved on the road to Manassas Junction, by order of General King, reaching the Junction at 7 a. m., having made a march of about 8 miles. After a short rest, which scarcely availed to refresh our weary and battle-worn soldiers, my brigade, together with the rest of the division, returned on the Centreville road again to a point about a mile east of the battle-field of the night before.

Here Jackson's army was drawn up to dispute the passage to Washington. King's division was posted on the left of General McDowell's line of battle. We remained in this position for two or three hours, when an order came for Hatch's and my brigades to attack the enemy's right, it being represented that his whole line was in great confusion, and that it was only necessary for us to move forward to render his rout complete and capture a large number of fugitives. Under this impression we advanced to the attack at the double-quick step, my brigade leading the way, accompanied by Captain Gerrish's battery. As we gained the crest of a hill the battery opened on the enemy, but without much effect, owing to their being well sheltered.

I have learned subsequently, from prisoners taken in the action, that we did not encounter Jackson's force at all. It was Longstreet's division, which had just come up, after having been delayed on its route from Thorougfare Gap by General Ricketts's command. Drawn up in three ranks, the front rank kneeling, the rebels poured in an incessant fire, their line not only confronting ours, but enveloping us on each flank. As their brigades came up one after another, while we received no re-enforcement, the contest soon became very unequal, and after reforming several times we were obliged to fall back, the enemy following, until checked by a daring charge of the Harris Light Cavalry, which ended the contest for the night. (Pages 269 and 270.)

[Report of Col. Thomas F. McCoy, One hundred and seventh Pennsylvania Infantry.]

OCTOBER 8, 1862.

* * * * * * *

At the dawn of the next morning (the 29th) we were again upon the road to Manassas, where we arrived before noon, and unexpectedly found it in the possession of our army. After two or three hours' rest the line of march was taken for another battlefield, the battle then raging with great fury near the old Bull Run battle-ground. At the close of the day we arrived upon the ground, the battle still in progress, the rebels being strongly pressed and yielding ground. The regiment, in connection with those composing the brigade, bivouacked on the field while the balls and shells of the enemy were still flying over and around them.

Soon after daylight the next morning (30th) the regiment was in line. (Page 387.)

[Report of General J. F. Reynolds, commander of third division.]

CAMP NEAR MUNSON'S HILL, VA., *September* 5, 1862.

* * * * * * *

I then returned to my own division, which I reached at daylight on the morning of the 28th [29th]; closed up with General Sigel's command on the old battlefield of Bull Run. General Sigel reported the enemy in his immediate front, and requested my co-operation with him in an attack upon his position. I accordingly formed my division on the left of General Sigel's corps, next to the division of General Schenck. General McDowell joined the command at daylight, and directed my co-operation with General Sigel.

The right of the enemy's position could be discerned upon the heights above Groveton, on the right of the pike. The division advanced over the ground to the heights above Groveton, crossed the pike, and Cooper's battery came gallantly into action on the same ridge on which the enemy's right was, supported by Meade's brigade. While pressing forward our extreme left across the pike, re-enforcements were sent for by General Sigel for the right of his line, under General Milroy, now hardly pressed by the enemy, and a brigade was taken from Schenck's command on my right. The whole fire of the enemy was now concentrated on the extreme right of my division, and, unsupported there, the battery was obliged to retire, with considerable loss in both men and horses, and the division fell back to connect with Schenck.

Later in the day General Pope, arriving on the right from Centreville, renewed the attack on the enemy and drove him some distance. My division was directed to threaten the enemy's right and rear, which it proceeded to do under a heavy fire of artillery from the ridge to the left of the pike. Generals Seymour and Jackson led their brigades in advance, but notwithstanding all the steadiness and courage shown by the men they were compelled to fall back before the heavy fire of artillery and musketry which met them both on the front and left flank, and the division resumed its original position. King's division engaged the enemy along the pike on our right, and the action was continued with it until dark by Meade's brigade. (Pages 393 and 394.)

[Report of Brig. Gen. George G. Meade, United States Army, commanding first brigade, of operations August 21 to September 4, including battles of Groveton and Bull Run.]

HEADQUARTERS FIRST BRIGADE, REYNOLDS'S DIVISION, P. R. V. C.,
Camp near Munson's Hill, Va., September 5, 1862.

CAPTAIN: I have to submit the following report of the operations of my command since leaving Fredericksburg on the night of August 21:

* * * * * * *

On the 29th the brigade was formed in line of battle on the left of Sigel's corps and directed to move on Gainesville. Sigel, having found the enemy on his front on the other side of the Warrenton pike, engaged them along his whole line, and the brigade moved up on his left until it crossed the Warrenton pike within a half mile of Groveton, at which point Cooper's battery was established on the ridge, with the Fourth, Seventh, and Eighth regiments to support him, the Third being posted along the pike and the Rifles sent up the pike as skirmishers.

The enemy, perceiving this disposition, brought several batteries to bear on Cooper's, who, being short of ammunition, was withdrawn, and Ransom's was about being substituted, when it was ascertained that Schenck's division of Sigel's corps, which had been on our right, was withdrawn, and at the same time the enemy's infantry were deploying in our front in such force as required the withdrawal of the brigade to the other side of the Warrenton pike, where a position was taken on the plateau near what is known as the Lewis House, which overlooks Groveton and the pike leading to it. This position was held until dark, when, ascertaining that the attack of a portion of King's division, on our right and front, had been repulsed and the enemy advancing in force, I directed the withdrawal of the batteries, and after dark withdrew the brigade to the position occupied by the rest of the division.

On the morning of the 30th the brigade advanced. (Pages 397 and 398.)

[Report of Maj. Gen. Samuel P. Heintzelman, United States Army, commanding Third Corps, Army of the Potomac, of operations August 14–September 2, including engagement at Kettle Run and battles of Groveton, Bull Run, and Chantilly.]

HDQRS. DEFENSES OF WASHINGTON SOUTH OF THE POTOMAC,
Arlington, Va., October 21, 1862.

* * * * * * *

At 10 a. m. I reached the field of battle, a mile from stone bridge, on the Warrenton turnpike. General Kearny's division had proceeded to the right and front. I learned that General Sigel was in command of the troops then engaged and called on him.

At 11 a. m. the head of Hooker's division arrived; General Reno an hour later. At the request of General Sigel I ordered General Hooker to place one of his brigades at General Sigel's disposal to re-enforce a portion of his line then hard pressed. General Grover reported, and before long became engaged, and was afterward supported by the whole division. General Pope arrived between 1 and 2 p. m. The enemy were driven back a short distance toward Sudley church, where they made another stand, and again pressed a portion of our line back. All this time General Kearny's division held its position on our extreme right. Several orders were sent to him to advance, but he did not move until after the troops on his left had been forced back, which was near 6 p. m. He now advanced and reported that he was driving the enemy. This was not, however, until after the renewed heavy musketry fire on our center had driven General Hooker's troops and those he was sent to support back. They were greatly outnumbered, and had behaved with exceeding gallantry.

It was on this occasion that General Grover's brigade made the most gallant and determined bayonet charge of the war. He broke two of the enemy's lines, but was finally repulsed by the overwhelming numbers in the rebel third line. It was a hand-to-hand conflict, using the bayonet and the butt of the musket. In this fierce encounter, of not over twenty minutes' duration, the Second New Hampshire, Colonel Marston, suffered the most. The First, Eleventh, and Sixteenth Massachusetts and Twenty-sixth Pennsylvania were engaged. The loss of this brigade, numbering less than two thousand present, was a total of four hundred and eighty-four, nearly all killed and wounded. I refer you to General Grover's accompanying report.

Had General Kearny pushed the enemy earlier, it might have enabled us to have held our center and have saved some of this heavy loss. Kearny on the right, with General Stevens and our artillery, drove the enemy out of the woods they had temporarily occupied. The firing continued until some time after dark, and when it ceased we remained in possession of the battlefield. During the night, however, our troops again fell back from the woods that had been so obstinately disputed all the afternoon. (Pages 412, 413.)

[Report of Brig. Gen. Philip Kearny, United States Army, commanding first division, of the battles of Groveton and Bull Run.]

HEDQRS. FIRST DIVISION, THIRD CORPS, ARMY OF THE POTOMAC,
Centreville, Va., August 31, 1862.

COLONEL: I report the part taken by my division in the battles of the two previous days. On the 29th, on my arrival, I was assigned to the holding of the right wing, my left on Leesburg road. I posted Colonel Poe, with Berry's brigade, in first line, General Robinson, first brigade, on his right, partly in line and partly in support, and kept Birney's most disciplined regiments reserved and ready for emergencies. Toward noon I was obliged to occupy a quarter of a mile additional on left of said road, from Schurz's troops being taken elsewhere.

During the first hours of combat General Birney, on tired regiments in the center falling back, of his own accord rapidly pushed across to give them a hand to raise themselves to a renewed fight. In early afternoon General Pope's order, per General Roberts, was to send a pretty strong force diagonally to the front to relieve the center in the woods from pressure. Accordingly I detached for that purpose General Robinson, with his brigade; the Sixty-third Pennsylvania Volunteers, Colonel Hays; the One hundred and fifth Pennsylvania Volunteers, Captain Craig; the Twentieth Indiana, Colonel Brown, and, additionally, the Third Michigan Marksmen, under Colonel Champlin.

General Robinson drove forward for several hundred yards, but the center of the main battle being shortly after driven back and out of the woods, my detachment, thus exposed, so considerably in front of all others, both flanks in air, was obliged to cease to advance, and confine themselves to holding their own. At 5 o'clock, thinking—though at the risk of exposing my fighting line to being enfiladed—that I might drive the enemy by an unexpected attack through the woods, I brought up additionally the most of Birney's regiments—the Fourth Maine, Colonel Walker and Lieutenant-Colonel Carver; the Fortieth New York, Colonel Egan; First New York, Major Burt, and One hundred and first New York, Lieutenant-Colonel Gesner—and changed front to the left, to sweep with a rush the first line of the enemy. This was most successful. The enemy rolled up on his own right. It presaged a victory for us all. Still our force was too light. The enemy brought up rapidly heavy reserves, so that our farther progress was impeded. General Stevens came up gallantly in action to support us, but did not have the numbers. (Pages 415, 416.)

[Reports of Brig. Gen. John C. Robinson, United States Army, commanding First Brigade, of engagement at Kettle Run and battles of Groveton, Bull Run, and Chantilly.]

HEADQUARTERS ROBINSON'S BRIGADE,
Centreville, Va., August 31, 1862.

CAPTAIN: I have the honor to submit the following report of the operations of my brigade yesterday and day before:

On Friday morning I was ordered to support Colonel Poe's brigade and to develop his line of battle to the right. After crossing Bull Run I moved forward in two lines—the first composed of the Twentieth Indiana and One hundred and fifth Pennsylvania, and the second of the Sixty-third Pennsylvania and five companies of the Thirtieth Ohio, which were temporarily attached to my command.

Arriving on the ground assigned me, I remained for a considerable time exposed to a heavy artillery fire, after which I took up my position on high ground farther to the right. I was soon after directed by Major-General Kearny, commanding division, to move to the support of Poe's left, when I formed the Sixty-third and One hundred and fifth Pennsylvania in line of battle on the Leesburg road, holding the Twentieth Indiana and Ohio battalion in reserve. At this time there was a heavy musketry fire to our left and front, and I was directed to move forward through the woods to turn the enemy and cut off his retreat through the railroad cut. On arriving on the ground with the Sixty-third and One hundred and fifth Pennsylvania, Twentieth Indiana, and Third Michigan, I found the railroad already occupied by our own troops and the cornfield in front filled with the enemy. I then deployed the Sixty-third and One hundred and fifth Pennsylvania along the railroad to the right of the troops in position, directing the Third Michigan to protect my right flank, placing the Twentieth Indiana in reserve, and throwing skirmishers to the front.

Soon after taking this position the regiments on my left gave way and passed rapidly to the rear out of the woods, leaving my left flank entirely exposed. As rapidly as possible I moved my command to the left to occupy the deserted ground, but before my troops could get fairly into position I was fiercely attacked by a superior force that had succeeded in crossing the road. I then threw forward my right wing, forming my line of battle at right angles to the original position, and checked the progress of the enemy. At this time General Birney brought up and turned over to me his Fourth Maine. He afterward sent me his First, Fortieth, and One hundred and first New York Regiments. These troops were deployed to the right and left of the railroad, and pushed forward to the support of my regiments in front, which were suffering severely from a terrific fire of musketry and the enemy's artillery, posted on a hill to our right and rear. Our men now gained steadily on the enemy, and were driving him before them until he brought up fresh masses of troops (supposed to be two brigades), when, with ammunition nearly expended, we withdrew to our second position. (Pages 421, 422.)

[Report of Brig. Gen. Cuvier Grover, United States Army, commanding first brigade, of engagement at Kettle Run and battles of Groveton and Bull Run.]

On the following day we recontinued our march for the plains of Manassas by the way of Centreville, and arrived upon the battlefield about 9 a. m. The battle had already commenced, and as my column moved to the front the shells fell with remarkable precision along the line of the road, but fortunately did no damage. My brigade was temporarily placed under the orders of Major-General Sigel, whose troops were then engaging the enemy in the center. Under instructions received from him I threw forward the First Massachusetts Volunteers to support his line, while my remaining four regiments were drawn up in two lines, sheltered from the enemy's fire by a roll of the field in front. This position was occupied until about 2.30 p. m.

In the mean time I rode over the field in front as far as the position of the enemy would admit. After rising the hill under which my command lay an open field was entered, and from one edge of it gradually fell off in a slope to a valley, through which ran a railroad embankment. Beyond this embankment the forest continued, and the corresponding heights beyond were held by the enemy in force, supported by artillery.

At 3 p. m. I received an order to advance in line of battle over this ground, pass the embankment, enter the edge of the woods beyond, and hold it. Dispositions for carrying out such orders were immediately made. Pieces were loaded, bayonets fixed, and instructions given for the line to move slowly upon the enemy until it felt his fire, then close upon him rapidly, fire one well-directed volley, and rely upon the bayonet to secure the position on the other side.

We rapidly and firmly pressed upon the embankment, and here occurred a short, sharp, and obstinate hand-to-hand conflict with bayonets and clubbed muskets. Many of the enemy were bayoneted in their tracks, others struck down with the buts of pieces, and onward pressed our line. In a few yards more it met a terrible fire from a second line, which in its turn broke. The enemy's third line now bore down upon our thinned ranks in close order, and swept back the right center and a portion of our left. With the gallant Sixteenth Massachusetts on our left I tried to turn his flank, but the breaking of our right and center and the weight of the enemy's lines caused the necessity of falling back, first to the embankment and then to our first position, behind which we rallied to our colors.

In this fierce encounter of not more than twenty minutes' duration our loss was as follows:

Command.	Killed.	Wounded.	Missing.	Total.
First Massachusetts Volunteers	5	66	7	78
Second New Hampshire Volunteers	16	87	30	183
Eleventh Massachusetts Volunteers	10	77	25	112
Sixteenth Massachusetts Volunteers	4	64	42	110
Twenty-sixth Pennsylvania Volunteers	6	33	14	53
	41	327	118	486

Though forced to retire from the field by the immensely superior numbers of the enemy, supported by artillery and by the natural strength of his position, men never fought more gallantly or efficiently. (Pages 438, 439.)

[Report of Brig. Gen. Nelson Taylor, United States Army, commanding second brigade, of engagement at Kettle Run and battles of Groveton and Bull Run.]

HEADQUARTERS SECOND BRIGADE, HOOKER'S DIVISION.
Camp near Fort Lyon, Virginia, September 8, 1862.

CAPTAIN: I have the honor to submit the following report of the movements and services rendered by the brigade from the 26th ultimo to the 3d instant inclusive:

* * * * * * *

The next morning (29th) the march was resumed, passing through Centreville. We arrived on the battle-ground about 2 p. m.

* * * * * * *

Having everything in readiness I gave the order to advance. The line had advanced but a few steps when the left was struck with such violence by a regiment (which continued the line to the left) which had broken, that the Second Excelsior Regiment, which was on the left of the brigade line, was almost carried away with it. Seeing the confusion, I rode hastily to this part of the line, accompanied by my two aids, Lieutenants Tremain and Dwight, and endeavored to stay this disgraceful retreat, but it was in vain; the tide could not be stemmed.
On they rushed over and through my line perfectly panic-stricken, breaking and carrying away with them the left of my line. The enemy seeing this charged after them. I then endeavored to throw back my line to give the enemy a flank fire. This I found on trial impracticable, the wood being too dense to execute the movement. By this time the enemy had availed themselves of the large interval opened on my left and poured through in large numbers, and had got 50 or 60 paces in my rear, giving the line an enfilading and reverse fire. They, however, soon ceased firing, as they were so mixed up as to endanger their own men; they then commenced taking prisoners. Finding my line completely flanked and turned, and in danger of being entirely cut off, I gave the order to fall back, which was done in as good order as could be, situated as we were. The loss on this occasion was not as large as I had reason to apprehend, yet it was considerable. (Pages 444 and 445.)

[Report of Capt. Charles L. Young, Seventieth New York Infantry, of engagement at Kettle Run and battles of Groveton and Bull Run.]

HDQRS. FIRST REGT., EXCELSIOR BRIG. (SECOND),
HOOKER'S DIV. (SECOND), THIRD ARMY CORPS,
Camp near Fort Lyon, Virginia, September 4, 1862.

LIEUTENANT: In compliance with orders from brigade headquarters I have the honor to report the part taken by this regiment in the recent battles at Bristoe Station, on the 27th, and Bull Run, on Friday and Saturday, August 29 and 30;

* * * * * * *

Left Union Mills August 29, at 3 a. m., reaching Centreville before 9 a. m., when we ascertained the enemy had made a stand beyond Bull Run. Our division was early ordered forward, reaching the field about noon. The first and third brigades were engaged first, the Excelsior (second) being held in reserve. Twice our position was changed, soon bringing us within supporting distance. The battle raged fearfully, the enemy making a desperate stand, never flinching. His artillery worked splendidly, exerting us to hold him in check. It soon became necessary to forward our brigade. Forming in line of battle facing a long wood, the Third Regiment on the extreme right, this command directly on their left and on the right of the other regiments of the brigade. with three regiments numbering twenty-four hundred strong immediately on the left of our brigade, we moved cautiously and steadily into the wood to relieve a force already engaging the enemy, who was behind and holding a railway.
We had barely time to reach the point designated when the rebels, with a murderous shout, accompanied by a sharp fire, broke through the brigade in front, forcing them pell-mell on our line of battle, at the same time skillfully turning our left flank and routing the brigade on our left from the wood, our men never wavering until Colonel Taylor saw it would be madness to expose his command to the mercies of a desperate and much larger foe. As it was, we held our ground until many of our mounted officers were dragged from their horses and our colors within the enemy's grasp. Still undaunted, Colonel Taylor rallied his little force at the edge of the wood that he might send skirmishers back

to protect the recovery of our wounded comrades, never leaving the field until the skirmishers had been twice driven in and orders arrived from General Hooker for us to retire. We passed the night on the top of a hill in the rear of a reserve battery. (Pages 446 and 447.)

[Report of Capt. H. J. Bliss, commanding Seventy-second New York Infantry.]

HEADQUARTERS THIRD REGIMENT,
Camp near Spring Hill, September 7, 1862.

I have the honor to report that the Third Excelsior, of your brigade, under my command, on the 29th of August took the position assigned on the right of the brigade line, and advanced into the timber, where a portion of our forces were already engaged with the enemy. My instructions were to halt behind the line engaged, and when their ammunition was exhausted take their place. I advanced skirmishers covering my whole front to this line and dressed my regiment accurately on the brigade line. Our position was hardly taken when the line of troops in our front, belonging to regiments never before under fire, gave way under a dashing attempt of the enemy to turn the left of our line. Gradually the left gave way, struggling hand-to-hand for life and their colors, until the line was broken up to the left of my command, rendered almost powerless by the influence and presence of the disorganized troops breaking through my line and preventing my firing until the enemy were actually in our ranks in overpowering numbers. We fell back 300 yards to the edge of the timber and again formed line and advanced skirmishers forward to the line we had just left. The enemy had also fallen back, and seemed unwilling to improve his temporary advantage. By order I again withdrew my skirmishers and subsequently took position for the night with the brigade. (Pages 451, 452.)

[Report of Col. Joseph B. Carr, Second New York Infantry, commanding third brigade, of operations August 15–30, including engagement at Kettle Run, and battles of Groveton and Bull Run.]

HEADQUARTERS THIRD BRIGADE, HOOKER'S DIVISION,
Camp near Fort Lyon, Va., September 6, 1862.

* * * * * * *

At 2 o'clock Friday morning, August 29, I received orders to march at 3 a. m. and support General Kearny, who was in pursuit of the enemy. A march of 10 miles brought us to the Bull Run battlefield. About 11 a. m. was ordered into position to support a battery in front of the woods, where the enemy was engaged with General Sigel's troops. Remaining about one hour in that position, was ordered to send into the woods and relieve two regiments of General Sigel's corps. I sent in the Sixth and Seventh New Jersey Volunteers. Afterward received orders to take the balance of the brigade into the woods, which I did at about 2 p. m. Here I at once engaged the enemy and fought him for a space of two hours, holding my position until our ammunition was all expended. About 4 o'clock we were relieved by General Reno and Colonel Taylor, but did not reach the skirt of the woods before a retreat was made and the woods occupied by the enemy. When I arrived out of the woods I was ordered to march about half a mile to the rear and bivouac for the night. (Pages 454, 455.)

[Report of Lieut. Col. William J. Sewell, Fifth New Jersey Infantry, of engagement at Kettle Run, and battles of Groveton and Bull Run.]

HEADQUARTERS FIFTH NEW JERSEY VOLUNTEERS,
Camp near Alexandria, Va., September 5, 1862.

* * * * * * *

SIR: I have the honor to make the following report of the part taken by the regiment under my command at the battle of Bull Run [Groveton], August 29:

I received orders to deploy my right wing as skirmishers in front of the brigade in an open wood. As soon as the line advanced to where the line of another division had previously been, firing commenced on both sides, continuing up to the time that the brigade was relieved. I was soon obliged to relieve my right with my left wing, the former having emptied their cartridge-boxes, containing sixty rounds. The men thus relieved I posted in the rear of the line of battle to prevent stragglers from leaving the fight. The brigade having been relieved by General Reno's brigade while I was forming the regiment, this last brigade fell back in disorder. I endeavored to stop them, but finding that the enemy were almost up to my line, deployed in the rear, and now being formed, having divided their cartridges equally, I saw that it was time for me to take care of my own command.

A part of the Eighth New Jersey, with their colors, formed on my left. The enemy having turned the left flank of the line of battle, came out in the open field on my left, and immediately after I received their fire from the front, which I returned, driving them from our immediate vicinity, and then marched to position on the right of the first line of the brigade, my left resting on the railroad. Advancing in this manner, I was soon entangled in a dense wood, which retarded my progress, it being almost impassable. I was obliged to halt several times and form the regiment. Skirmishers in advance reporting the enemy in my immediate vicinity, the Second New York and One hundred and fifteenth Pennsylvania, on my left, soon became engaged. Finding it impossible to push my way through the woods in anything like order, I threw one company to the left of the railroad and one across the track. Three companies immediately opened a flank fire on the enemy, who were using the high embankment of the railroad as a breastwork. After a few volleys the enemy gave way, when I ordered a charge up the railroad. The regiment advanced on the double-quick, the enemy running before us.

At this point I took one prisoner, who was not able to keep up with his comrades. Halting in an open field, on the brow of a hill, the enemy in sight on my left and front, the regiment rested until the rest of the brigade came up. The infantry did not again become engaged.

Later in the day I was ordered to picket a road 2 miles to the left. While performing this duty the regiment captured twenty-three prisoners.

* * * * * * *

In this engagement the officers and men of the regiment, without any exceptions, behaved with great gallantry. All seemed to be actuated with the same spirit, and that was to fight.

[Report of General R. E. Lee, C. S. A.]

June 8, 1863.

* * * * * * *

Generals Jones and Wilcox bivouacked that night east of the mountain, and on the morning of the 29th the whole command resumed the march, the sound of cannon at Manassas announcing that Jackson was already engaged. Longstreet entered the turnpike near Gainesville, and moving down toward Groveton, the head of his column came upon the field in rear of the enemy's left, which had already opened with artillery upon Jackson's right, as previously described. He immediately placed some of his batteries in position, but before he could complete his dispositions to attack the enemy withdrew, not, however, without loss from our artillery. Longstreet took position on the right of Jackson, Hood's two brigades, supported by Evans, being deployed across the turnpike and at right angles to it. These troops were supported on the left by three brigades under General Wilcox and by a like force on the right under General Kemper. D. R. Jones's division formed the extreme right of the line, resting on the Manassas Gap Railroad. The cavalry guarded our right and left flanks, that on the right being under General Stuart in person.

After the arrival of Longstreet the enemy changed his position and began to concentrate opposite Jackson's left, opening a brisk artillery fire, which was responded to with effect by some of General A. P. Hill's batteries. Colonel Walton placed a part of his artillery upon a commanding position between the lines of Generals Jackson and Longstreet by order of the latter and engaged the enemy vigorously for several hours. Soon afterward General Stuart reported the approach of a large force from the direction of Bristoe Station, threatening Longstreet's right. The brigades under General Wilcox were sent to re-enforce General Jones, but no serious attack was made, and after firing a few shots the enemy withdrew. While this demonstration was being made on our right a large force advanced to assail the left of Jackson's position, occupied by the division of General A. P. Hill. The attack was received by his troops with their accustomed steadiness and the battle raged with great fury. The enemy was repeatedly repulsed, but again pressed on to the attack with fresh troops. Once he succeeded in penetrating an interval between General Gregg's brigade, on the extreme left, and that of General Thomas, but was quickly driven back with great slaughter by the Fourteenth South Carolina Regiment, then in reserve, and the Forty-ninth Georgia, of Thomas's brigade.

The contest was close and obstinate, the combatants sometimes delivering their fire at ten paces. General Gregg, who was most exposed, was re-enforced by Hays's brigade, under Colonel Forno, and successfully and gallantly resisted the attacks of the enemy until, the ammunition of his brigade being exhausted and all his field officers but two killed or wounded, it was relieved, after several hours of severe fighting, by Early's brigade and the Eighth Louisiana Regiment. General Early drove the enemy back with heavy loss, and pursued about 200 yards beyond the line of battle, when he was recalled to the position on the railroad where Thomas, Pender, and Archer had firmly held their ground against every attack. While the battle was raging on Jackson's left General Longstreet ordered Hood and Evans to advance, but before the order could be obeyed Hood was himself attacked, and his command at once became warmly engaged. General Wilcox was recalled from the right and ordered to advance on Hood's left, and one of Kemper's brigades, under Colonel Hunton, moved forward on his right. The enemy was repulsed by Hood after a severe contest and fell back, closely followed by our troops.

The battle continued until 9 p. m., the enemy retreating until he reached a strong position, which he held with a large force. The darkness of the night put a stop to the engagement, and our troops remained in their advanced position until early next morning, when they were withdrawn to their first line. One piece of artillery, several stands of colors, and a number of prisoners were captured.

HEADQUARTERS ARMY OF NORTHEASTERN VIRGINIA,
Chantilly, Va., September 3, 1862.

MR. PRESIDENT: My letter of the 30th ultimo will have informed your excellency of the progress of this army to that date. General Longstreet's division, having arrived the day previous, was formed in order of battle on the right of General Jackson, who had been engaged with the enemy since morning resisting an attack commenced on the 28th. The enemy on the latter day was vigorously repulsed, leaving his numerous dead and wounded on the field. His attack on the morning of the 29th was feeble, but became warmer in the afternoon, when he was again repulsed by both wings of the army; his loss on this day, as stated in his published report, herewith inclosed, amounting to eight thousand killed and wounded. (Page 559.)

[Report of Lieut. Gen. James Longstreet, C. S. Army, commanding First Corps, of operations August 16–September 2, including battles of Groveton and Manassas, &c.]

HEADQUARTERS, NEAR WINCHESTER, VA., *October* 10, 1862.

GENERAL: I have the honor to submit the following report of the operations of my command in the late campaign:

* * * * * * *

Early on the 29th the columns were united and the advance to join General Jackson was resumed. The noise of battle was heard before we reached Gainesville. The march was quickened to the extent of our capacity. The excitement of battle seemed to give new life and strength to our jaded men, and the head of my column soon reached a position in rear of the enemy's left flank and within easy cannon-shot. On approaching the field some of Brigadier-General Hood's batteries were ordered into position, and his division was deployed on the right and left of the turnpike at right angles with it, and supported by Brigadier-General Evans's brigade. Before these batteries could open the enemy discovered our movements and withdrew his left. Another battery (Captain Stribling's) was placed upon a commanding position to my right, which played upon the rear of the enemy's left and drove him entirely from that part of the field. He changed his front rapidly, so as to meet the advance of Hood and Evans. Three brigades, under General Wilcox, were thrown forward to the support of the left, and three others, under General Kemper, to the support of the right, of these commands.

General D. R. Jones's division was placed upon the Manassas Gap Railroad to the right and *en échelon* with regard to the three last brigades. Colonel Walton placed his batteries in a commanding position between my line and that of General Jackson, and engaged the enemy for several hours in a severe and successful artillery duel. At a late hour in the day Major-General Stuart reported the approach of the enemy in heavy columns against my extreme right. I withdrew General Wilcox, with his three brigades, from the left and placed his command in position to support Jones in case of an attack against my right. After some few shots the enemy withdrew his forces, moving them around toward his front, and about 4 o'clock in the afternoon began to press forward against General Jackson's position. Wilcox's brigades were moved back to their former position, and Hood's two brigades, supported by Evans, were quickly pressed forward to the attack. At the same time Wilcox's three brigades made a like advance, as also Hunton's brigade, of Kemper's command. These movements were executed with commendable zeal and ability.

Hood, supported by Evans, made a gallant attack, driving the enemy back until 9 o'clock at night. One piece of artillery, several regimental standards, and a number of prisoners were taken. The enemy's entire force was found to be massed directly in my front, and in so strong a position that it was not deemed advisable to move on against his immediate front; so the troops were quietly withdrawn at 1 o'clock the following morning. The wheels of the captured piece were cut down and it was left on the ground.

The enemy seized that opportunity to claim a victory, and the Federal commander was so imprudent as to dispatch his Government by telegraph tidings to that effect. After withdrawing from the attack my troops were placed in the line first occupied and in the original order. (Pages 564, 565.)

[Report of Maj. Gen. David R. Jones, C. S. Army, commanding division, of operations August 15–September 2.]

RICHMOND, VA., *December* 8, 1862.

MAJOR: I have the honor to submit the following report of the movements of my division and of the part it performed in the engagements of the campaign in Northern Virginia and Maryland. Serious illness and absence from the field has delayed its appearance till now.

* * * * * * *

Crossing the Rappahannock River, I reached Thoroughfare Gap on the 28th, and under orders from General Longstreet sent forward the Ninth Georgia Regiment, Anderson's brigade, into the Gap, following it with my whole division.

* * * * * * *

Appearances indicating his retreat, I advanced my command and bivouacked beyond the Gap unmolested by the enemy. The intense darkness and ignorance of the fords over the creek in my front prevented pursuit.

* * * * * * *

Early on the morning of the 29th I took up the line of march in the direction of the old battle-ground of Manassas, whence heavy firing was heard. Arriving on the ground about noon, my command was stationed on the extreme right of our whole line, and during the balance of the day was subjected to shelling, resulting in but few casualties.

On the morning of the 30th slight alterations were made in the disposition of my command, throwing it more forward and to the right, the battle meanwhile raging fiercely on the left. (Page 579.)

[Reports of Brig. Gen. Cadmus M. Wilcox, C. S. Army, commanding division, of skirmish at Kelly's Ford and battle of Manassas.]

HEADQUARTERS ANDERSON'S DIVISION,
October 11, 1862.

* * * * * * *

Early the following morning our march was resumed, and the command rejoined at 9.30 a. m. the remainder of the division at the intersection of the two roads leading from the gaps above mentioned. Pursuing our line of march, together with the division, we passed by Gainesville, and advancing some 3 miles beyond, my three brigades were formed in line of battle on the left and at right angles to the turnpike. Having advanced near three-fourths of a mile, we were then halted. The enemy was in our front and not far distant. Several of our batteries were placed in position on a commanding eminence to the left of the turnpike A cannonading ensued and continued for an hour or two, to which the enemy's artillery replied.

At 4.30 or 5 p. m. the three brigades were moved across to the right of the turnpike a mile or more to the Manassas Gap Railroad. While here musketry was heard to our left on the turnpike. This firing continued with more or less vivacity till sundown. Now the command was ordered back to the turnpike and forward on this to the support of General Hood, who had become engaged with the enemy and had driven him back some distance, inflicting severe loss upon him, being checked in his successes by the darkness of the night. After reaching General Hood's position but little musketry was heard; all soon became quiet. Our pickets were thrown out to the front. The enemy's camp fires soon became visible, extending far off to our left, front, and right. Remaining in this position till 12 o'clock at night, the troops were withdrawn three-fourths of a mile to the rear and bivouacked, pickets being left to guard our front. (Page 598.)

[Report of Brig. Gen. John B. Hood, C. S. Army, commanding division, of operations August 22–31, including Freeman's Ford, Groveton, and Manassas.]

DIVISION HEADQUARTERS, *September* 27, 1862.

* * * * * * *

After a spirited little engagemedt with them by General D. R. Jones's troops, on the evening of the 28th instant, our forces were able to bivouac for the night beyond the Gap.

The next morning at daylight the march was agained resumed, with this division in the advance, Lieutenant-Colonel Upton, of the Fifth Texas, in command of a party of select Texan riflemen, constituting the advance guard. Coming up with the rear guard of the enemy before sunrise, this gallant and distinguished officer drove them before him so rapidly that halts would have to be made for the troops in rear to rest.

Early in the day we came up with the main body of the enemy on the plains of Manassas, engaging General Jackson's forces. Disposition of the troops being made, the Texas brigade advanced in line of battle down and on the immediate right of the pike leading to the stone bridge, and Colonel Law's brigade on the left. Arriving on a line with the line of battle established by General Jackson, the division was halted by order of the general commanding.

About 4 o'clock in the afternoon the enemy made a fierce attack upon General Jackson, his noble troops holding their ground with their usual gallantry. At sunset an order came to me from the commanding general to move forward and attack the enemy. Before, however, this division could come to attention it was attacked, and I instantly ordered the two brigades to move forward an charge the enemy, which they did most gallantly, driving them in confusion in front of them. Colonel Law's brigade, being engaged with a very heavy force of the enemy, captured one piece of artillery, three stand of colors, and one hundred prisoners, and the Texas brigade three stand of colors. It soon became so very dark that it was impossible to pursue the enemy any farther.

At 12 o'clock at night orders came to retake our position on the right of General Jackson, in which we remained until 4 o'clock the next afternoon, August 30, when the battle of the plains of Manassas commenced. (Page 605.)

[Report of Col. P. F. Stevens, commanding Evans's Brigade.]

HDQRS. HOLCOMBE LEGION, SOUTH CAROLINA VOLS,
Near Winchester, Va., October 13, 1862.

* * * * * * *

On August 29, after a fatiguing day's march, my regiment, with the rest of the brigade, was put in line of battle in support of General Hood's brigade. The line was scarcely formed when the order was given, "Forward." The obscurity of the hour caused me to separate from the brigade; but I moved forward until within a few yards of the enemy's camp-fires. I was met by a messenger, who assured me that the camp was already occupied by a Texas regiment. Halting, I sent a messenger to report to General Evans. (Page 630.)

[Report of Lieut. Gen. Thomas J. Jackson, C. S. Army, commanding Second Corps, of operations August 15-September 3.]

HDQRS. SECOND CORPS, ARMY OF NORTHERN VIRGINIA,
April 27, 1863.

GENERAL: I have the honor herewith to submit to you a report of the operations of my command from August 15 to September 5, 1862, embracing the several engagements of Manassas Junction, Bristoe Station, Ox Hill, and so much of the battle of Groveton (on August 28, 29, and 30) as was fought by the troops under my command:

* * * * * * *

The next morning (29th) I found that he had abandoned the ground occupied as the battlefield the evening before and had moved farther to the east and to my left, placing himself between my command and the Federal capital. My troops on this day were distributed along and in the vicinity of the cut of an unfinished railroad (intended as a part of the track to connect the Manassas road directly with Alexandria), stretching from the Warrenton turnpike in the direction of Sudley's mill. It was mainly along the excavation of this unfinished road that my line of battle was formed on the 29th—Jackson's division, under Brigadier-General Starke, on the right, Ewell's division, under Brigadier-General Lawton, in the center, and Hill's division on the left.

In the morning, about 10 o'clock, the Federal artillery opened with spirit and animation upon our right, which was soon replied to by the batteries of Poague, Carpenter, Dement, Brockenbrough, and Latimer, under Major [L. M.] Shumaker. This lasted for some time, when the enemy moved around more to our left to another point of attack. His next effort was directed against our left. This was vigorously repulsed by the batteries of Braxton, Crenshaw, and Pegram.

About 2 p. m. the Federal infantry in large force advanced to the attack of our left, occupied by the division of General Hill. It pressed forward, in defiance of our fatal and destructive fire, with great determination, a portion of it crossing a deep cut in the railroad track and penetrating in heavy force an interval of nearly 175 yards, which separated the right of Gregg's from the left of Thomas's brigade. For a short time Gregg's brigade, on the extreme left, was isolated from the main body of the command; but the Fourteenth South Carolina Regiment, then in reserve, with the Forty-ninth Georgia, left of Colonel Thomas, attacked the exultant enemy with vigor and drove them back across the railroad track with great slaughter. General McGowan reports that the opposing forces at one time delivered their volleys into each other at the distance of 10 paces. Assault after assault was made on the left, exhibiting on the part of the enemy great pertinacity and determination, but every advance was most successfully and gallantly driven back.

General Hill reports that six separate and distinct assaults were thus met and repulsed by his division, assisted by Hays's brigade, Colonel Forno commanding.

By this time the brigade of General Gregg, which from its position on the extreme left was most exposed to the enemy's attack, had nearly expended its ammunition. It had suffered severely in its men, and all its field officers except two were killed or wounded. About 4 o'clock it had been assisted by Hays's brigade (Colonel Forno). It was now retired to the rear to take some repose after seven hours of severe service, and General Early's brigade, of Ewell's division, with the Eighth Louisiana Regiment, took its place. On reaching his position General Early found that the enemy had obtained possession of the railroad and a piece of wood in front, there being at this point a deep cut, which furnished a strong defense. Moving through a field he advanced upon the enemy, drove them from the wood and railroad cut with great slaughter, and followed in pursuit some 200 yards; the Thirteenth Georgia at the same time advanced to the railroad and crossed with Early's brigade. (Pages 645 and 646.)

[Report of Maj. Gen. Ambrose P. Hill, commanding second division, of operations August 20 to September 2.]

HEADQUARTERS LIGHT DIVISION,
Camp Gregg, Virginia, February 25, 1863.

* * * * * *

Friday morning, in accordance with orders from General Jackson, I occupied the line of the unfinished railroad, my extreme left resting near Sudley Ford, my right near the point where the road strikes the open field, Gregg, Field, and Thomas in the front line, Gregg on the left, and Field on the right, with Branch, Pender, and Archer as supports. My batteries were in the open field in rear of the infantry, the nature of my position being such as to preclude the effective use of much artillery. The evident intention of the enemy this day was to turn our left and overwhelm Jackson's corps before Longstreet came up, and to accomplish this the most persistent and furious onsets were made by column after column of infantry, accompanied by numerous batteries of artillery. Soon my reserves were all in, and up to 6 o'clock my division, assisted by the Louisiana brigade of General Hays, commanded by Colonel Forno, with a heroic courage and obstinacy almost beyond parallel, had met and repulsed six distinct and separate assaults, a portion of the time the majority of the men being without a cartridge.

The reply of the gallant Gregg to a message of mine is worthy of note: "Tell General Hill that my ammunition is exhausted, but that I will hold my position with the bayonet." The enemy prepared for a last and determined attempt. Their serried masses, overwhelming superiority of numbers, and bold bearing made the chances of victory to tremble in the balance: my own division exhausted by seven hours' unremitted fighting, hardly one round per man remaining, and weakened in all things save its unconquerable spirit. Casting about for help, fortunately it was here reported to me that the brigades of Generals Lawton and Early were near by, and sending to them they promptly moved to my front at the most opportune moment, and this last charge met the same disastrous fate that had befallen those preceding. Having received an order from General Jackson to endeavor to avoid a general engagement, my commanders of brigades contented themselves with repulsing the enemy and following them up but a few hundred yards.

During the night of the 29th my brigades were engaged in refilling cartridge boxes and generally putting themselves in condition for the morrow's fight. (Pages 670, 671.)

[Report of Brig. Gen. Samuel McGowan, C. S. Army, commanding Gregg's brigade.]

HEADQUARTERS SECOND BRIGADE, A. P. HILL'S LIGHT DIVISION,
Camp Gregg, Virginia, February 9, 1863.

* * * * * * *

We slept upon our arms near Ewell's battlefield, and the next morning at early dawn returned near the position first taken up by us the evening before, and were placed in line of battle on the extreme left of the whole command near Catharpin Run. We occupied a small, rocky, wooded knoll, having a railroad excavation bending around the east and north fronts and a cleared field on the northwest. This position was slightly in advance of the general line, and besides being on the extreme left, was considered important because of the

Sudley Ford road, which it commanded. Our line made an obtuse angle, pointing toward the enemy, one side of which ran nearly parallel with the railroad cut and the other along the fence bordering the cleared field before spoken of. Within these contracted limits was the little tongue of woodland which we occupied, and which we were directed to hold at all hazards.

On this spot, barely large enough to hold the brigade, we stood and fought with intervals of cessation from 8 o'clock in the morning until dark. We repulsed many successive charges, I believe seven, the enemy constantly throwing fresh columns upon us, and persisting in his effort to carry the point with the utmost obstinacy. During the different struggles of the day the regiments were relieved and shifted as occasion required. The space covered by the brigade was so small and the distance between the regiments so inconsiderable that I would not be able, if it were necessary, to state all the movements which were made. I can only advert to the positions of the respective regiments at one or two important junctures during the day.

* * * * * * *

It was now 4 p. m., and there was no abatement in the fury of the assaults, when the brigades of Generals Branch and Early, having been sent to our assistance, came in most opportunely and gallantly. After these re-enforcements had arrived and passed to the front General Gregg collected the remnant of his regiments, and, placing them in line behind the troops now engaged, gave them instructions to lie down, and if our friends were overpowered and had to fall back over them to wait until the enemy was very near, then rise and drive them back at the point of the bayonet. The men all lay down as instructed, resolved as the last resort to try the virtue of the cold steel, but happily the necessity did not arise. The enemy were finally driven back at all points, and night closed upon us occupying the identical spot which we were ordered to hold in the morning.

We slept on the field of battle and remained in position all the next day, while the great battle of the Second Manassas was progressing on our right. The enemy made several attempts to advance, but the admirable practice of Captain McIntosh's battery kept them beyond musket-range, scattering them with shot and shell every time they moved forward. Some few men were wounded by shell, but we were not very actively engaged on that day.

Friday, the 29th, was the glorious but bloody day for the brigade. (Pages 680, 681.)

[Report of Brig. Gen. James J. Archer, Confederate States army, commanding brigade, of operations August 24–September 2.]

HEADQUARTERS ARCHER'S BRIGADE,
Camp Gregg, near Fredericksburg, Va., March 1, 1863.

MAJOR: I have the honor to present the following report of the operations of my brigade in the series of battles from Warrenton Springs Ford to Shepherdstown, inclusive:

* * * * * * *

About 4 p. m., during an interval of the assaults of the enemy, General Pender sent his aid-de-camp, requesting me to relieve him, and with the consent of General Hill, who was near me at the time, I immediately marched down and filed to the right into the railroad cut. As my leading files entered the railroad cut I perceived the enemy advancing up it from the left into the wood. Unwilling to commence the fight until my troops were in position, I did not call their attention to the enemy until half of my last regiment (Colonel Turney's, First Tennessee) had entered the cut. I then pointed out the enemy on the left and ordered that regiment to fire, which it did with great effect. The first fire of this regiment was instantly answered by a furious assault upon my whole front.

At this time my own brigade was the only one in sight along the whole line, but for twenty minutes or more it firmly and gallantly resisted the attack and maintained its position until other troops came on my right and left in time to save me from being flanked. Soon after the arrival of these fresh troops we charged and drove the enemy back several hundred yards, and then quietly returned to our position. In a few minutes fresh forces of the enemy arrived and attacked us as vigorously as the first. They were as firmly resisted and as gallantly repelled by another charge. At this second charge many of my men were out of ammunition, and charged with empty rifles. I did not average over two cartridges to the man. A third assault was met and repulsed in the same manner, my brigade charging upon the enemy with loud cheers and driving them back with their empty rifles.

It was after sunset when we resumed our position, and we lay upon our arms that night with a strong picket in front to prevent surprise. (Page 699, 700.)

[Report of Maj. Gen. James E. B. Stuart, C. S. Army, commanding cavalry of the Army of Northern Virginia, of operations August 16 to September 2.]

HDQRS. STUART'S CAV. DIV., ARMY OF N. VA.,
February 28, 1863.

GENERAL: I have the honor to furnish the following summary of events in which my command participated immediately preceding and subsequent to the second battle of Manassas, or, as it should be more properly termed, the battle of Groveton Heights, August 30, 1862:

* * * * * * *

The next morning (29th), in pursuance of General Jackson's wishes, I set out again to endeavor to establish communication with Longstreet, from whom he had received a favorable report the night before. Just after leaving the Sudley road my party was fired on from the woods bordering the road, which was in rear of Jackson's lines and which the enemy had penetrated with small force, it was afterward ascertained, and captured some stragglers. They were between General Jackson and his baggage at Sudley.

I immediately sent to Major [W.] Patrick, whose six companies of cavalry were near Sudley, to interpose in defense of the baggage and use all the means at hand for its protection, and ordered the baggage at once to start for Aldie. General Jackson, also being notified of this movement in his rear, sent back infantry to clear the woods. Captain Pelham, always at the right place at the right time, unlimbered his battery and soon dispersed that portion in the woods. Major Patrick was attacked later, but he repulsed the enemy with considerable loss, though not without loss to us, for the gallant major, himself setting the example to his men, was mortally wounded. He lived long enough to witness the triumph of our arms, and expired thus in the arms of victory. The sacrifice was noble, but the loss to us irreparable.

I met with the head of General Longstreet's column between Hay Market and Gainesville, and there communicated to the commanding general General Jackson's position and the enemy's. I then passed the cavalry through the column, so as to place it on Longstreet's right flank, and advanced directly toward Manassas, while the column kept directly down the pike to join General Jackson's right. I selected a fine position for a battery on the right, and one having been sent to me, I fired a few shots at the enemy's supposed position, which induced him to shift his position. General Robertson, who with his command was sent to reconnoiter farther down the road toward Manassas, reported the enemy in his front. Upon repairing to that front I found that Rosser's regiment was engaged with the enemy to the left of the road and Robertson's vedettes had found the enemy approaching from the direction of Bristoe Station toward Sudley.

The prolongation of his line of march would have passed through my position, which was a very fine one for artillery as well as observation, and struck Longstreet in flank. I waited his approach long enough to ascertain that there was at least an army corps, at the same time keeping detachments of cavalry dragging brush down the road from the direction of Gainesville, so as to deceive the enemy—a ruse which Porter's report shows was successful—and notified the commanding general, then opposite me on the turnpike, that Longstreet's flank and rear were seriously threatened, and of the importance to us of the ridge I then held. Immediately upon receipt of that intelligence Jenkins's, Kemper's, and D. R. Jones's brigades and several pieces of artillery were ordered to me by General Longstreet, and, being placed in position fronting Bristoe, awaited the enemy's advance. After exchanging a few shots with rifle pieces, this corps withdrew toward Manassas, leaving artillery and supports to hold the position until night. (Pages 735, 736.)

From these official reports I gather the following facts as to

THE FORCES ENGAGED,

the duration of the battle, the character of the conflict, and the losses in men:

First. At the battle of Groveton, August 29, 1862, we have seen from the official reports that there were engaged:

1. UNION.

1. Sigel's entire corps, three divisions, all day.
2. Reno's, small division, Ninth Corps, from 10 o'clock.
3. Heintzelman's corps, two divisions, from about 10 o'clock.
4. McDowell's corps, two divisions, during evening.

Total, four corps, eight divisions.

2. CONFEDERATES.

General T. J. Jackson's corps: General Taliaferro's division, General A. P. Hill's division, General Ewell's (Lawton's) division, all day.

General James Longstreet's corps: General Wilcox's division, General Hood's division, General Kemper's division, (Hunton's brigade), last part of day.

General Jones watching Porter.

Total, two corps, six divisions.

DURATION OF CONFLICT.

Second. The time engaged:

General Pope says it "lasted with continuous fury from daylight until after dark." "Shortly after daylight Sigel and Reynolds's divisions of McDowell's corps had become engaged." "Darkness closed the action on Friday."

General Sigel says: "Formed in order of battle at daybreak." "From 6.30 to 10.30 in the morning our whole infantry force and nearly all our batteries were engaged." "At 10.30 the enemy threw forward large masses of infantry." "Major-General Kearny arrived on the field of battle and deployed by the Sudley Springs road on our right." "General Reno's troops came to our support by the Gainesville turnpike." "The contest began with renewed vigor and vehemence, the enemy attacking furiously along the whole line." "At 2 o'clock in the afternoon General Hooker's troops arrived on the field of battle, and were immediately ordered forward by their noble commander into battle." "During two hours, from 4 to 6 p. m., strong cannonading and musketry continued on our center and right." "At 6.15 Brigadier-General King's division of Major-General McDowell's corps arrived behind our front and advanced on the Gainesville pike."

Schenck says: "On Friday morning early the engagement was commenced by General Milroy on our right, in which we soon took part." "We remained here nearly an hour, the firing in the mean while becoming heavy on the right."

Schurz says: "On the 29th, a little after 5 o'clock a. m., you ordered me to cross the turnpike, to deploy my division north of it, and attack the forces of the enemy." "Meanwhile the fire in front had extended along the whole line and become very lively." "It was about 10 a. m., when an officer announced to me that General Kearny had arrived on the battlefield." "My troops, who had started at 5 o'clock in the morning, mostly without breakfast, had been under fire for eight hours." "Re-enforcements arrived in my front between 1 and 2 o'clock." "Worn down as my men were, my division was unable to take part in the action after 2 o'clock p. m."

Milroy says: "The following morning, the 29th, at daylight I was ordered to proceed in search of the rebels." "The enemy now [p. m.] came on in overwhelming numbers. General Carl Schurz had been obliged to retire with his two brigades an hour before." "When the storm was raging fiercest General Stahel came to me and reported," &c. "Toward evening General Grover came up with his New England brigade."

McDowell says: "I received your instructions to order the division over to the north of the turnpike to support the line held by Reno, which had been hotly engaged all day. It was now near dusk, and though the men had now been on foot since 1 o'clock in the morning, they moved forward with the greatest enthusiasm."

Hatch says: "Late on the afternoon of the 29th I was ordered by General McDowell in person to move the division on the Gainesville road in pursuit of the enemy," &c. "The struggle, lasting some three-quarters of an hour, was a desperate one. Night had now come on."

Colonel McCoy, commanding first brigade, Ricketts's division, says: "At the dawn of the next morning, the 29th, we were again upon the road to Massassas." "At the close of the day we arrived upon the ground, the battle still in progress." "Bivouacked on the field, while the balls and shells of the enemy were still flying over and around them."

Reynolds says: "The action was continued with it until dark by Meade's brigade."

Heintzelman says: "At 10 a. m. I reached the field of battle." "At 11 the head of Hooker's division arrived; General Reno an hour later." "General Grover reported, and before long became engaged." "The firing continued until some time after dark."

Kearny says: "During the first hours of the combat General Birney pushed across," &c. "In the early afternoon General Pope's order, per General Roberts, was to send a pretty strong force diagonally to the front," &c. "At 5 o'clock * * * I brought up the most of Birney's regiments * * * to sweep with a rush the enemy's first line."

Grover says: "Arrived on the battlefield about 9 a. m." "The battle had already commenced." "At 3 p. m. I received an order to advance in line of battle."

Carr says: "About 11 a. m., ordered into position." "Received orders to take balance of brigade into woods, which I did about 2 p. m.; here I engaged the enemy and fought him for a space of two hours." "About 4 o'clock we were relieved by General Reno."

Either there is a vast amount of lying in these reports, or else Pope was about right when in his dispatch to Halleck, written during that night and sent at 5 o'clock next morning, he said the battle "lasted with continuous fury from daylight until after dark."

I will now introduce some witnesses whom our friends on the other side will scarcely dispute, because they are certainly disinterested witnesses so far as this question is concerned.

R. E. Lee says: "On the morning of the 29th the whole command resumed the march, the sound of cannon announcing that Jackson was already engaged. Engaged the enemy vigorously for several hours. The battle continued until 9 p. m."

Longstreet says: "The noise of battle was heard before we reached Gainesville. Hood supported by Evans made a gallant attack, driving the enemy back until 9 o'clock at night."

Hood says: "About 4 o'clock in the afternoon, the enemy made a fierce attack on General Jackson. It soon became so dark that it was impossible to pursue the enemy farther."

Jackson says: "About 10 o'clock the Federal artillery opened. About 2 o'clock the Federal infantry advanced."

Hill says: "Up to 6 o'clock my division * * * had met and repulsed six distinct and separate assaults."

McGowan says: "We stood and fought with intervals of cessation from 8 o'clock in the morning until dark."

THIRD. AS TO THE CHARACTER OF THE BATTLE.

Lee says: "The battle raged with great fury." "The enemy was repeatedly repulsed, but again pressed on to the attack with fresh troops." "The contest was close and obstinate." "The enemy was repulsed by Hood after a severe contest."

Jackson says: "It [Federal infantry] pressed forward in defiance of our fatal and destructive fire with great determination." "Assault after assault was made." "Six separate and distinct assault were thus met and repulsed."

A. P. Hill says: "The enemy prepared for a last and determined attempt. Their serried masses, overwhelming superiority of numbers, and bold bearing made the chances of victory to tremble in the balance." "My own division, exhausted by seven hours' unremitted fighting."

McGowan says: "We repulsed many successive charges; I believe seven."

Archer says: "The first fire of this regiment was answered by a furious assault on my whole front."

General Pope says: "We fought a terrific battle." "Lasted with continuous fury." "The action raged furiously all day."

General Sigel says: "The contest began with renewed vigor and vehemence, the enemy attacking furiously along the whole line."

General Schurz says: "The enemy made another furious charge upon my center." "I then ordered a general advance of my whole line, which was executed with great gallantry."

General Milroy says: "My brave lads were dashed back before the storm of bullets like chaff before the tempest."

General McDowell says: "The attack was severe both on the enemy and on our men."

General Hatch says: "The struggle * * * was a desperate one, being in many instances a hand-to-hand conflict."

Colonel McCoy says: "The battle then raging with great fury." "The rebels being strongly pressed and yielding ground."

Reynolds says: "Compelled to fall back before the heavy fire of artillery and musketry which met them."

General Meade says: "The renewed heavy musketry fire on our center had driven General Hooker's troops."

Heintzelman says: "The most gallant and determined bayonet charge of the war."

Kearny says: "General Robinson drove forward for several hundred yards, but the center of the main battle being shortly after driven back," &c.

Robinson says: "My regiments which were suffering from a terrific fire of musketry and the enemy's artillery."

Grover says: "An obstinate hand-to-hand conflict with bayonets and clubbed muskets." "Met a terrific fire from a second line, which in its turn broke."

Captain Young says: "The battle raged fearfully, the enemy making a desperate stand, never flinching."

If this engagement is to be judged by the desperate and unflinching character of the conflict, which delivers and withstands seven successive assaults, which empties cartridge-boxes of 60 rounds of cartridge, then this was a great battle.

FOURTH. LOSSES IN THE BATTLE OF AUGUST 29, 1862.

Return of casualties in the Union forces, commanded by Maj. Gen. John Pope during the operations August 16–September 2, 1862, inclusive.

Command.	Killed.		Wounded.		Captured or missing.		Aggregate.
	Officers.	Enlisted men.	Officers.	Enlisted men.	Officers.	Enlisted men.	
Army of Virginia	63	866	245	4,144	67	2,720	8,105
Army of the Potomac	54	546	172	2,841	27	1,088	4,728
Ninth Army Corps	15	189	43	957	11	308	1,523
Kanawha division (detachment).	....	14	1	49	1	41	106
Grand total	132	1,615	461	7,991	106	4,157	14,462

This includes all the fighting on the Rappahannock, the battles at Catlett's 25th, Kettle Run 26th and 27th, Manassas 26th and 27th, Bull Run Bridge 27th, Thoroughfare Gap and Gibbon's fight 28th, Groveton 29th, Bull Run 30th, and Chantilly September 1, and nearly one-half that entire loss was on the 29th, at Groveton.

I believe that it is demonstrable that one-half of this entire loss occurred upon the 29th.

The loss of Sigel's corps was two thousand and eighty-seven, nearly all upon the 29th. The loss of McDowell's corps was five thousand four hundred and sixty-nine, of which fully one-half was on the 29th. The loss of Heintzelman's corps was two thousand two hundred and thirty-eight, by far the greater part on the 29th. The total loss of Porter's corps was two thousand one hundred and fifty-one, all but three on the 30th. The total loss of Sykes's division during entire period, nine hundred and eighteen, of which four hundred and twelve was from Warren's little brigade, leaving five hundred and six for the rest of the division, including three batteries. Morell's loss, one thousand two hundred and thirty-three, of which five hundred and seventy-six was in Roberts's brigade; five hundred and ninety in Butterfield's brigade.

These figures are taken from the official reports of The War of the Rebellion.

The loss of the 29th could not have fallen short of six thousand killed and wounded.

Pope says: "We have lost not less than eight thousand men killed and wounded." (Dispatch 5 a. m., August 30, from field of battle.)

"Our loss during that day was not less than six thousand or eight thousand killed and wounded, and I think this estimate will be confirmed by the general reports which cover the losses. (Report, September 3, 1862.)

Schurz says: "My troops * * * had been decimated by enormous losses."

Milroy says: "I rallied the shattered remnant of my brigade."

Hatch (King's division) says: "Our loss had been severe."

Heintzelman says: "The loss of this brigade (Grover's), numbering less than two thousand present, was a total of four hundred and eighty-four, nearly all killed and wounded."

Robertson says: "Our loss in this action was severe, embracing some of our best officers. The enemy's loss must have been very great."

General R. E. Lee says: "Our loss was severe in this engagement. His (Pope's) loss on this day (29th), as stated in his published report herewith inclosed, amounting to eight thousand killed and wounded."

SUMMARY.

From these official reports it appears that the forces engaged on the 29th consisted of eight divisions of the Union Army and six divisions of the confederate army, comprising the best fighting material of both armies (if Porter's corps be excepted). If the divisions be estimated at five thousand each only, that would make forty thousand on the Union side and thirty thousand on the confederate side. In fact Jackson alone had twenty-two thousand men.

These armies were under the immediate command of Lee and Pope, the commanding generals, assisted by such generals as Jackson, Longstreet, McDowell, Hooker, and Kearney. The battle continued from sunrise until after dark. It "raged with continuous fury." The losses were not less than six thousand on the Union side, and Generals Hooker and Kearney, two good fighters, estimated that the confederate loss was greater. And yet the Schofield board and General Grant base the reversal of the finding of the court-martial upon the supposed fact that there was no battle upon the 29th.

I have recently read the Personal Memoirs of General Grant, including his history of the so-called Mexican war, and his account of certain so-called "battles." It has been considered something of a war; yet the losses in battle of General Scott from Vera Cruz to the city of Mexico, and, I believe, in that entire war, were less than the losses of the Union Army on the 29th of August, 1862.

There has been an impression abroad that there was a battle fought at Bunker Hill in 1775. Yet the American losses on that day in killed, wounded, and missing were only four hundred and fifty-two—less than the loss in Grover's Brigade alone on the 29th in a single charge.

There has been a popular superstition abroad that a "battle" was fought at Bull Run on the 21st of August, 1861, under the command of Beauregard on the one side and McDowell on the other. Yet the entire loss of the Union Army on that day was but two thousand nine hundred and fifty-two, of which about one thousand was in prisoners, or, in other words, the killed and wounded were about one-third the killed and wounded on the 29th of August, 1862. And yet, in the face of these well-known and incontrovertible facts, the defense and restoration of Fitz-John Porter is made to hinge upon the claim that there was no battle upon the 29th of August, 1862.

I do not believe that in all the history of civil or military trials so astounding a proposition was ever before advanced. There are probably living to-day forty thousand men who took part in that battle.

We shall next be told that there was no civil war; that there was a "labor riot" in Gettysburg, a "strike" at Vicksburg, and the sheriff's posse succeeded in arresting the rioters at Appomattox. [Applause and laughter.] I am about ready to believe with the Berkeleian philosophy, that there is no external world, and therefore no history;

that life and so-called events are simply a series of internal impressions, with no corresponding external pheuomena. [Laughter.] The keystone of the arch of Porter's defense having fallen, the whole arch tumbles about the heads of those who support it. [Continued applause.]

FIFTH. DID PORTER KNOW THERE WAS A BATTLE?

If he did he was not to blame for it. He stopped just as far from it as he could, and then went 2½ miles from the head of his own column, back behind a hill, and laid down in the woods, 5 miles from the main battle and 4 miles from the nearest fighting. But even there the sounds of battle reached him. We know this beyond question from his own dispatches to McDowell at the time.

General Porter reported to General McDowell his views and intentions in the following dispatches:

Generals McDowell and King:

I found it impossible to communicate by crossing the woods to Groveton. The enemy are in great force on this road, and as they appear to have driven our forces back, the fire of the enemy having advanced and ours retired, I have determined to withdraw to Manassas. I have attempted to communicate with McDowell and Sigel, but my messengers have run into the enemy. They have gathered artillery and cavalry and infantry, and the advancing masses of dust show the enemy coming in force. I am now going to the head of the column to see what is passing and how affairs are going, and I will communicate with you. Had you not better send your train back?

F. J. PORTER, *Major-General.*

General McDowell or King: I have been wandering over the woods and failed to get a communication to you. Tell how matters go with you. The enemy is in strong force in front of me, and I wish to know your designs for to-night. If left to me, I shall have to retire for food and water, which I can not get here. How goes the battle? It seems to go to our rear. The enemy are getting to our left.

F. J. PORTER,
Major-General Volunteers.

General McDowell: The firing on my right has so far retired that, as I can not advance and have failed to get over to you except by the route taken by King, I shall withdraw to Manassas. If you have anything to communicate, please do so. I have sent many messengers to you and General Sigel and get nothing.

F. J. PORTER,
Major-General.

(Report Schofield board, volume 12, page 2, War of Rebellion.)

McDowell's testimony (page 85, G. C. M.):

Was or not the battle raging at that time? [while Porter and McDowell were together at Dawkin's Branch about 12 m.].

A. The battle was raging on our right.

Col. E. G. Marshall, who was one of Porter's chief witnesses both on the court-martial and before the board and who commanded Porter's skirmish line that day, testified before the court as follows:

About the same time, before I went in to General Morell, I could hear and judge of the result of the fighting between the force of the enemy and General Pope's army. I could see General Pope's left and the enemy's right during the greatest part of the day about 2 miles off, perhaps more, diagonally to our front and right. The enemy set up their cheering, and appeared to be charging and driving us, so that not a man of my command but what was certain that General Pope's army was being driven from the field.

He goes on to describe how he could distinguish "the enemy's yell when they are successful," which he describes as "a continual yelling." I presume that may bring it vividly to the minds and memory of many of us.

Porter knew there was a battle, and fully believed it was going against Pope.

WHEN DID LONGSTREET ARRIVE,

and was his whole corps present?

General D. R. Jones had forced the passage of Thoroughfare Gap on the night of the 28th and "bivouacked beyond [east of] the gap." Jones led the advance on the 29th. He says he arrived on the ground "about noon."

Col. P. F. Stevens, commanding Evans's brigade, Hood's division (which came up next after Jones), says: "On August 29, after a fatiguing day's march, my regiment, with the rest of the brigade, was put in line of battle to support Hood's brigade. The line was scarcely formed when the order was given, 'forward.' The obscurity of the hour caused me to separate from the brigade." So it must have been quite late when Evans's brigade arrived.

William M. Owen (adjutant, Washington Artillery): "Marched to Groveton at the head of the column, directly after the escort of Lee and Longstreet. Reached the battlefield at 11.30 a. m." (Schofield board, page 552.)

At noon on the 29th, the two batteries in reserve, having halted near *the village of Gainesville*, 3 miles from field, on the Warrenton and Centreville turnpike, were ordered forward by General Longstreet to engage the enemy, then in our front and near the village of Groveton. Captains Miller and Squires at once proceeded to the position indicated by the general and opened fire upon the enemy's batteries." (Major Walton, commanding Washington Artillery, volume 12, page 2, page 571.)

We may also approximate the arrival of Lee and Longstreet from J. E. B. Stuart's report (War of Rebellion, volume 12, part 2, page 740), as follows:

Friday, August 29, as General Stuart rode forward toward Groveton, about 10 a. m., he found that the enemy's sharpshooters had penetrated the woods, going toward the ambulances and train, threatening to cut them off. He at once directed Captain (now Major) Pelham, of the Stuart Horse Artillery, who was near by, to shell the woods and gather up all the stragglers around the train and drive back the enemy. Notifying General Jackson in the mean time of what was transpiring, he also ordered the quartermaster to move the train toward Aldie, and sent an order to Major Patrick to keep his battalion of cavalry between the enemy and the baggage train, a duty which he faithfully discharged, receiving a mortal wound just as he gallantly and successfully repulsed a large force of the enemy that was attempting to cross the run. General Stuart also sent to Colonel Baylor, who was near the railroad embankment, in command of the Stonewall Brigade, asking him to come forward and drive back the enemy; but he replied, "I was posted here for a purpose, and have positive orders to stay here, which I must obey."

Having ordered Captain Pelham to report to General Jackson, General Stuart went toward Hay Market to establish communication with Generals Lee and Longstreet, accompanied by Brigadier-General Robertson with a portion of his and portion of General Fitzhugh Lee's cavalry. General Stuart met Generals Lee and Longstreet on the road between Hay Market and Gainesville, and informed them of what had happened and the situation of General Jackson's forces and those of the enemy. General Lee inquired for some way to the Sudley road. General Stuart showed him that the best route for them was by the turnpike, which they took, and General Stuart moved to Longstreet's right flank. The detachment of cavalry under General Fitzhugh Lee that had been to Burke's Station returned in the p. m. of this day to the vicinity of General Jackson, at Sudley.

The night of Friday, August 29, General Stuart was 2 miles east of General Longstreet's command.

The attack was made on Jackson's train "about 10 a. m." near Sudley Ford. Stuart remained there until the attack was repulsed; rode toward Hay Market. Stuart met Lee and Longstreet between Hay Market and Gainesville. After leaving Sudley he must have ridden with his column at least 6 miles. He met Lee and Longstreet at the head of their column, communicated the situation, then passed his cavalry division—about two thousand cavalry—through the column, and went to the right toward Manassas.

This would give us this time-table: Attack on train, 10 a. m.; repulsed in, say, one-half hour, 10.30 a. m.; ride to Hay Market, 6 miles, say, one hour, 11.30 a. m.; interview with Lee and passing a division of cavalry through column, one hour, 12.30 p. m. (see Longstreet in February Century); march of Longstreet's infantry from point where Stuart met him to point where line was formed, at Pageland lane, 3½ miles, one and one-half hours, 2 p. m.

General Thomas L. Rosser swears (Schofield board, page 1073):

> Longstreet's command was coming in a very forced and disordered march from the direction of Thoroughfare Gap, moving rapidly and straggling badly.

How long would it require to close up in mass and deploy into line of battle say twenty-four thousand troops, "coming in a very forced and disordered march, straggling badly?" I apprehend that four divisions of infantry, with artillery, ammunition trains, and other *impedimenta*, would occupy not less than from two to two and one-half hours in closing up and getting into line of battle. That would bring us to 4 p. m. or 4.30 p. m.

Colonel Marshall, in his testimony before the court, swore that Longstreet's force "continued to come down all day; in fact, until 1 o'clock at night."

From all this I draw the conclusion that Lee, personally, arrived at Gainesville, 3 miles from the battle, at about noon; that by 1 o'clock the Washington Artillery (at the head of the column) reached the vicinity of Jackson's right, near Pageland lane; that by 2 o'clock the head of Longstreet's infantry began to go into line on the turnpike; that they were arriving all the afternoon; that Evans's brigade of Hood's division did not arrive until near night; that Longstreet's forces continued to arrive through the night; that the only force of Longstreet's troops within 2 miles of Porter up to 4.30 was D. R. Jones's and a small force of cavalry; that if Porter had moved promptly on arriving at Dawkin's Branch he could have seized the Monroe Hill and prevented the union of Lee and Jackson that afternoon.

The troops which Porter first encountered in front of Dawkin's Branch and near the Randall house were no part of Longstreet's command, but were two regiments of Jubal A. Early's brigade of Ewell's division of Jackson's corps.

Early, in his letter to Porter, under date of February 23, 1874 (proceedings Schofield board, Senate Ex. Doc. 37, Forty-sixth Congress, page 553), says:

> On the morning of the 29th I was ordered by Jackson to take a position on his right and about 1 mile from his main body with my own and Hays's Louisiana brigades, * * * in order to watch a body of Federal troops reported to be moving up from the direction of Manassas Junction. * * * Two regiments of my brigade were detached by General Jackson and placed southeast of the Warrenton pike in the direction of Manassas from my main position for the purpose of observing and reporting the approach of the opposing force. * * * Early in the day my two advanced regiments began skirmishing with the advance of the force coming from the direction of Manassas.

(See also testimony of General Early, Schofield board, page 810 [850.])

Now, we know that there was no other force "coming from the direction of Manassas" that day on that road but Porter's command. The only force in front of him then on his arrival at his most advanced point was two regiments of Early's brigade and the cavalry outposts. If he had promptly deployed a brigade, supported by another, instead of halting at Dawkin's Branch, he ought to have had possession of the Hampton Cole and Britt's ridge in thirty minutes. He would then have been in communication with Reynolds's left, and if forced to fall back would have fallen back to his right, and reunited Pope's army. This was his order. This order he disobeyed. The result was the crushing repulse of Reynolds and Hatch that evening between sundown and 9 o'clock.

I think that I have demonstrated, if anything in human history is capable of demonstration, that

THERE WAS A GREAT BATTLE UPON THE 29TH;

that Porter knew it from the sounds of battle; that he fully believed that the battle was going against Pope and the Union Army; that he did stand from noon until 9 o'clock at night, when the battle ceased, across the right flank of the enemy—first of Jackson (Early's brigade), and later, after the middle of the afternoon, D. R. Jones, of Longstreet (with twelve thousand or more men); that he did not attack—that he did not even demonstrate with any force or vigor; that he never attempted to advance his line across Dawkin's Branch; that he made no energetic attempt of any kind to communicate with Pope's right wing; that during most of this time he was more than two miles from the head of his own troops, exhibiting the least possible concern as to what was the fate of the day, except he had a constantly recurring desire to withdraw to Manassas. Manassas was toward Alexandria, and at Alexandria was McClellan. At Groveton was the battle, and in the battle was Pope.

But where did General Grant get his idea that there was no battle on the 29th? Not from the official reports, manifestly. He appears never to have read them; they are not mentioned among his three days' reading. Not from the evidence taken before the court-martial. It nowhere appears that he read that. Not from the evidence taken before the Schofield board. He asked for that in his letter of December 23, 1881, after he had announced his decision. He did have Schofield's report, and in that report we find the following:

> The judgment of the court-martial upon General Porter's conduct was evidently based upon greatly erroneous impressions, not only respecting what that conduct really was and the orders under which he was acting, but also respecting all the circumstances under which he acted. Especially was this true in respect to the character of the battle of the 29th of August.
>
> * * * * * * *
>
> The reports of the 29th and those of the 30th of August have somehow been strangely confounded with each other. Even the confederate reports have, since the termination of the war, been similarly misconstrued. Those of the 30th have been misquoted as referring to the 29th, thus to prove that a furious battle was going on while Porter was comparatively inactive on the 29th. The fierce and gallant struggle of his own troops on the 30th has thus been used to sustain the original error under which he was condemned. General Porter was, in effect, condemned for not having taken any part in his own battle. Such was the error upon which General Porter was pronounced guilty of the most shameful crime known among soldiers. We believe not one among all the gallant soldiers on that bloody field was less deserving of such condemnation than he.

It was from this report that General Grant drew his facts, a most unsafe source from which to derive facts. That report was made expressly to acquit. If the facts did not fit that end, then so much the worse for the facts.

Now what was the origin of and how much was there of this

ALLEGED CONFUSION OF THE 29TH WITH THE 30TH?

The facts are simply as follows: After Porter made his appeal to President Grant in 1869 General McDowell obtained from the confederate archives in charge of the War Department extracts from the official reports of Longstreet, Stuart, and Jackson, and sent them in the form of printed slips to General Pope, then in command of the Department of the Lakes. General Pope was preparing a reply to Porter's statement under the title of "A brief view," and as he designed using some of the extracts, he forwarded them to General Ed. Schriver, Inspector-General, and confidential secretary to the Secretary of War, with the request that he would verify the extracts as true extracts from the official reports in question for the operations of the 29th August, 1862. General Schriver replied under date of 7th January, 1870, saying:

I am now able to inclose the printed extracts from the rebel commanders' reports of engagements certified to by the Adjutant-General.

Mr. BRAGG. Will the gentleman permit me to correct him?

Mr. CUTCHEON. Certainly.

Mr. BRAGG. The certificate that was appended to that circular which was made by the Adjutant-General did not have any heading. McDowell placed upon it a heading, "Operations 29th day of August." So that your witnesses certified to a falsehood, and distributed it over the United States as evidence by which to convict.

Mr. CUTCHEON. It was certified by the Adjutant-General to be a correct copy of the records on file in the War Department.

One of these extracts was a brief portion of the report of General T. J. Jackson, which was supposed to relate to the charge of General Grover's brigade on the afternoon of the 29th, but which, upon the publication of the entire report subsequently, proved to relate to the charge of Butterfield's brigade over the same ground on the 30th. The extract was as follows:

After some desultory skirmishing and heavy cannonading during the day, the Federal infantry, about 4 o'clock in the evening, moved from under cover of the wood and advanced in several lines, first engaging the right, but soon extending its attack to the center and left. In a few moments our entire line was engaged in a fierce and sanguinary struggle with the enemy. As one line was repulsed another took its place and pressed forward as if determined by force of numbers and fury of assault to drive us from our positions. So impetuous and well sustained were these onsets as to induce me to send to the commanding general for re-enforcements, but the timely and gallant advance of General Longstreet on the right relieved my troops from the pressure of overwhelming numbers and gave to those brave men the chances of a more equal conflict. As Longstreet pressed upon the right the Federal advance was checked, and soon a general advance of my whole line was ordered. Eagerly and fiercely did each brigade press forward, exhibiting in parts of the field scenes of close encounter and murderous strife not witnessed often in the turmoil of battle. The Federals gave way before our troops, fell back in disorder, and fled precipitately, leaving their dead and wounded on the field. During their retreat the artillery opened with destructive power upon the fugitive masses. The infantry followed until darkness put an end to the pursuit.

The similarity of the assaults upon Jackson's line upon the afternoons of the 29th and 30th as to time, place, and character of the assault is exceedingly remarkable. The first was made by Hooker's troops, the one on the 30th was made by Porter's troops. This error made by the Adjutant-General in regard to this one brief extract was and is the only "confusion" that has ever arisen at any time in regard to the battles of the 29th and 30th of August, 1862. I boldly challenge the denial or refutation of this statement.

The Schofield report clearly carries the implication that this confusion in some way affected the judgment of the court-martial. But when it is considered that at the time of General Porter's conviction and sentence nothing whatever was known of the confederate reports, and that this error did not occur until seven years afterward, and was immediately corrected, it will be seen how preposterous and how false to fact this supposition is.

As General Grant himself says, his remarks as to Porter's justification "would not apply if a battle had been raging between Jackson and Pope."

I HAVE PROVED THAT A BATTLE WAS RAGING,

and therefore by his own judgment his statements do not apply.

The four conditions on which General Grant says he condemned Porter are shown to have existed. They were proved before the court-martial to have existed.

Not lightly, not impulsively, not from prejudice, not malignantly did such men as Hunter and Hitchcock and Garfield cast the ballots that under any other government in the world would have condemned Porter to death. Not heedlessly nor callously did the great and kind-hearted Lincoln put his approval to the sentence.

Since this case was last before Congress, Hon. Leonard Swett, one of President Lincoln's most intimate friends, sent to the Chicago Tribune an account of an interview which he had with Mr. Lincoln when the case of General Fitz-John Porter was before him for the approval of the court-martial's verdict. The President pointed to a pile of manuscripts lying on the table, with the remark that that was the record of the case, adding: "You know that if I know anything it is what evidence tends to prove and when a thing is proved. I have read every word in that record, and I tell you Fitz-John Porter is guilty and ought to be shot."

Not lightly did Abraham Lincoln condemn any man to disgrace and obloquy, and least of all one whom but shortly before he had promoted to a major-general for his services at Malvern Hill.

Garfield condemned him. He of the full-orbed brain and tender spirit, he whose strong and logical mind went to the bottom of every question which duty called him to investigate and understand. He condemned him upon the court-martial. Himself a soldier, with all the high sense of honor of a soldier, knowing well the duty of a soldier, after seeing the witnesses face to face, after seeing and hearing the accused, and all that he had to urge in extenuation or defense, he voted for his conviction. Year after year went by, Porter made appeal after appeal; he brought forward his so-called new evidence from confederate sources; but

GARFIELD SAW NO REASON TO CHANGE HIS JUDGMENT

of the case. When the Schofield board met, he watched the evidence with all the keenness and penetration of his trained and acute intellect, but he saw no cause to believe that the court-martial had erred. In February, 1880, just a few months before his nomination to the Presidency, he wrote to his friend, General J. D. Cox:

> I have been so stung by the decision of the Schofield board that it is very hard to trust my own mind to speak of it as it appeared to me.

Mr. Chairman, the argument is almost closed. The die is cast, the tale is almost told. The decree of the highest military tribunal ever assembled upon this continent, and the executed order of the martyr President, are about to be sponged out. I apprehend, judging the future by the past, that neither argument nor evidence will change the result. Though

Hunter, and Hitchcock, and Garfield, and Lincoln were to come forth from their charnel house and again declare him "guilty," I am persuaded that it would change no vote on the other side of this House. Those are not the names you conjure with. Though the thousands slain, who fell by reason of Porter's blind prejudice, his unfaithfulness to his country's trust, and his insubordination to the superior whom his Government had placed over him, were to come forth from their resting place on yonder heights at Arlington and file in ghostly procession before you, and with the stony lips of death pronounce him guilty of their sacrifice, and "plead trumpet-tongued against the deep damnation of their taking off," this bill would still be passed. The fiat has gone forth that Fitz-John Porter must be "vindicated."

Ah! gentlemen, you may pass this bill. You may affix the stigma of imbecility or malignity to the court that tried him. You may restore him to the rolls of that Army made illustrious by deeds of immortal valor and purest patriotism. You may elevate him over the heads of all the gray-haired veteran officers who never swerved from the line of patriotic devotion and loyal obedience. You may erase the word "guilty" where Garfield wrote it, and inscribe in its place the words "not guilty." Where Lincoln wrote "approved," you may wipe off the word and write over it "disapproved," but it is beyond your power to vindicate Fitz-John Porter. This is not the forum nor these the voices that have the power to change

THE VERDICT OF HISTORY.

God forbid, Mr. Chairman, that I, or any of us, should stand here against an act of justice, or of mercy even, from any bitterness of a past strife, or worse yet, from any excess of party zeal. If I am conscious of my own motives, neither of these does move me. I have given to the consideration of this case long and careful study, and all the power of analysis and all the maturity of judgment of which I am possessed. In the light of that study and that analysis of evidence, I see as in a vision the events of that long sultry August afternoon. I stand at the head of Porter's column while within cannon-range the dusty-gray column of the enemy presses eagerly down across his front upon the worn-out and shattered battalions of the Union army. I hear the summons of the cannon—the same that Longstreet's men heard—calling him to the glorious fray for the cause of Union, liberty, and law. I see the reeling, wavering lines as they advance or recede with the ever-fluctuating tide of batte. I hear the shrill, far-reaching yells of the enemy as they sweep down upon our lines, and the "old glory" of the Union goes down before the resistless sweep.

It would seem as if every drop of blood in his veins, every sentiment of honor, truth, and loyalty should have impelled him with resistless power to the field of battle. But no! In listless ease, careless of the fate of his commander, his comrades, and his country, he listens to the receding roar of the conflict, and proposes to retire to Manassas without lifting hand or foot for the rescue.

Mr. Chairman, it is not for me to judge for others, not for me to say how others shall cast their votes; but as for myself, when the roll shall be called which shall decide whether the word "approved" where it was written by the hand of Lincoln shall be sponged off, my answer must be, no. [Loud and prolonged applause.]

www.ingramcontent.com/pod-product-compliance
Lightning Source LLC
Chambersburg PA
CBHW022156020726
47496CB00008B/2750
9783337401740